❧ No more magic?

Chris isn't too sure about that. Especially after Halloween night when his bike mysteriously disappears. It was an old bike—not the kind somebody would be likely to steal. And Chris had always felt it was somehow special, almost magical.

As he begins to investigate, Chris finds that other strange things have been happening in town. Like Muffin's warlock costume being stolen, and *somebody* showing up at Chris's house wearing it. Muffin is convinced that these events are all connected . . . and that finding the bike will lead to her missing parents.

Chris's mother and father keep saying there's a logical explanation for everything. And his older brother Mike is just as bad, with his super-scientific approach. So it's up to Chris and Muffin to discover what's *really* going on.

Just about everyone is under suspicion for a while . . . including Muffin, who nobody really knows much about. But at last the evidence seems to fall neatly into place—or does it? *No more magic?* Maybe. Maybe not.

No More Magic

Avi

No More Magic

Pantheon Books

Library of Congress Cataloging in Publication Data

Avi, 1937– No more magic.
SUMMARY: While searching for his bicycle that disappeared on
Halloween, a young boy and his two friends become involved in a
magic adventure.   [1. Magic—Fiction.   2. Mystery and detective
stories]   I. Title.   PZ7.A953No3   [Fic]   74-15299   ISBN
0-394-83084-9 ISBN 0-394-93084-3 (lib. bdg.)   0 9 8 7 6 5 4 3 2 1

Designed by Cathy Goldsmith
Manufactured in the United States of America.

For Kevin

No More Magic

❧ Right after school

I met my best friend, Eddie. Eddie's a neat guy. He's the best drawer in class and knows just as much about super-heroes as I do. Maybe more. I know more about magic. We get together and do some great things. I had my Green Lantern suit and he was going to get his Batman costume. That's why we met. It was Halloween that night.

Now you have to understand that in my town Halloween is a big thing. The kind of costume you wear is pretty important and you've got to protect your secret identity. If anything, most of the fun is faking out your friends as to who you are.

We got on our bikes and headed out of town up

toward Eddie's house two miles away. We had decided to work on our costumes in secret at the swimming hole by the old bridge, which is close to his place. It was a Friday afternoon, kind of cold too, so I had to wear my old black-and-white checkered jacket. We got up there fast.

I had brought my stuff that morning so I didn't have to go home. While I laid out my costume, he rode on to get his. He came back running all the way. That's how excited we were.

His costume was really great, with gray tights and a fantastic mask which his mother had helped him to make. He even had boots, black ones, and a Batrope. I was sure he'd win the prize for the best costume at the Halloween parade that night.

My costume was good too. My mother had given me a real green ring which if you held it just right kind of glowed. My father had found a mask which was perfect. I made the rest myself.

When we got our stuff on we played around for a while, working out a story about how Batman and the Green Lantern were fighting Magic Marvel. (I made him up.) It was a cool game. I kept thinking up magic tricks which Magic Marvel played on us, while Eddie thought up ways to get out of his evil traps. In the end we got him. We usually do.

When we had finished we wanted to show off our costumes to someone. Eddie had the idea of sneaking up to his house through the woods to surprise his folks. That's just what we did.

Leaving the road, we climbed up the hill pretending that we were taking a secret trail. But there was no trail in the woods and we kept tripping. Branches were slapping at us, and it began to get dark. For a moment Eddie lost his way and had to stop and look around.

"I can hear you breathing," I said.

"I can hear you."

In the silence there was a crashing noise back somewhere. I stopped and I tried to see what had caused the sound. Eddie tried too.

"Nothing, probably," he finally said, then started to push on again. I had to hurry to catch up.

It wasn't too long before we had snuck up to his place and burst into the kitchen where his parents were. I think they were surprised, even a little frightened. Not that they admitted it. Anyway, they liked the costumes.

By that time it was pretty dark so Rosemary, Eddie's mother, drove me home in time for supper. My folks were a little annoyed because I hadn't told them where I was going. But as soon as they saw that

I had been at Eddie's house and that his mother had been around, they forgot about me, and invited Eddie's parents for dinner or something.

When my brother Mike—he's my older brother —saw my costume, he admitted it was pretty good, but he didn't think I would fool anybody. But then, he teases me a lot about the magical stuff I make up. With him, everything has to be scientific, real. "You wouldn't catch me dead in a costume," he let me know.

I remember that afternoon so well because it was the last time things were ordinary for a while. That night the town was crawling with ghosts, goblins, witches—and other weird stuff. But things really began when I looked outside the next morning, Saturday, and discovered that my bike wasn't there.

And by the way, my name is Chris.

∞ "Stupid," I said out loud, for I knew right away that it was my own fault for having left it out on Halloween night. My mind had been on too many other things, my Green

Lantern suit for one. That was why it had happened. I just forgot about it.

I should describe the bike. My folks got it for me on my birthday, just the month before, so I could learn to ride, which I did—cinchy.

A two-wheeler, it didn't have any gears or fancy stuff, just a regular handlebar, seat, and basket. It wasn't new. In fact, some kids used to make fun of it, said my folks got it in a junk yard, which was sort of true.

Still, I liked it. It had a shimmery green color which I had never seen on any other bike. Sometimes I liked to think it glowed in the dark, or that it had some kind of magical powers. That's because I think of green as magical.

When I saw it packed behind some stuff in Mr. Bullen's junk yard I knew it was the one I wanted, even though Mr. Bullen said it wasn't as good as a yellow bike he had. But I liked that green color. The Green Lantern and all. That's the bike that was stolen from me.

Dressing as quickly as I could, I ran outside without even eating breakfast. It was still pretty early. Nobody was on the street. The houses, which are sort of old and bunched up right next to each other, looked cold and empty with their window shades down. Most of the trees didn't have any leaves left and reminded me of kids just out of the shower, shivery.

I was hoping that my father had put the bike in the toolshed, or that my mother had moved it to the side alley, or that Mike had borrowed it. They had all done those things before. But just looking at the empty street I knew it was gone. Our place is pretty small, a six-room brick house with a small yard, so there aren't many hiding places. I checked. It was nowhere. Stolen.

I went in for breakfast. My mother had gone to work. My brother was in his room working on his radio things. My father was cleaning up breakfast. I sat down at our table and just stared at nothing.

"Want something to eat?" my father asked me, sort of letting me know I was late.

"Yes, thank you," I answered, using the "thank you" as a kind of apology which he accepted without a word.

I brought in a bowl and a cup, while he carried the cereal and milk. I ate alone, not saying anything. My father didn't seem to notice that I was upset, just went about his work. But when he was done, he suddenly said, "What's up?"

"Nothing," I told him, not ready to admit what I had done.

"Sure?" he asked again.

"Well, my bike's gone." It really was too much to keep to myself.

"Forget to put it away last night?"

"Guess so," I answered, in a way that let him know *that* was not the important part. Then I had a thought. "Did you put it somewhere to teach me a lesson?"

"Nope."

"Did Ma?"

"I doubt it, but you can call her and find out."

I wasn't going to do that because one, I would just be asking for criticism, and two, if she had put it away, I would have found it.

"What about Mike?" my father suggested.

"Working on his radio stuff. Besides, he wouldn't do that."

For a moment my father didn't say anything. "You picked a bad night to leave it out," he told me, as if I didn't know. Then he added, "When you're finished, we better go look for it."

I cleaned up my breakfast things, made my bed, put on a sweater, and then went up to my father's room which is on the top floor, to tell him I was ready.

He put down his book—he's always reading— got on his jacket and we went out to look.

I live in a big town, or a small city, depending on the way you look at it. They say there are four thousand people living here, but most people seem to know each other. Least they act that way. That's not to say bad things don't happen. Bikes get stolen and all that. Still, it's only a sometimes thing, and mostly people blame outsiders. If a bike is taken it's hard to keep it hidden. There are lots of houses, but nobody has fences.

My father and I went up and down our street a few times on both sides. We checked the empty lot on York Street. We went by Mr. Fason's Bar and behind the busted-down stable. My father asked Ted Black, Mr. Fason's helper, and then Ike, who lives at the corner, if they had seen it. They hadn't. I asked Richard and Roger if they had. Nothing. The Green brothers, who know everything that's going on, hadn't noticed a thing. When we asked Mrs. Hack—she's the old lady who lives right across the street—she gave me a cookie. It was good, but it didn't help find the bike.

We spent almost a whole hour but didn't find one trace.

"Let's go inside and talk it over," my father suggested. Feeling cold, I was glad to agree.

He made some cocoa to get us warm and while

it was on the stove he called my mother. She's a weaver and was at her studio, but she knew nothing either.

Over hot drinks we talked about what might have happened.

"Okay," said my father. "You left it out, right?" Only that time he wasn't accusing me of anything, just trying to get the facts straight.

"That's right," I agreed.

Then—and it was just the way he did things—he pulled out pencil and paper and suggested we put all the facts down.

My father's a librarian, works at the State College not far from town, which means he spends a lot of time studying, writing, and reading. If there is one thing he says, it's "Get the questions right before you get the answers wrong." I think he's said that six million times.

So, right at the top of the paper, he wrote—WHO STOLE THE BIKE?

Under that he wrote—FACT NUMBER ONE: IT WAS LEFT OUTSIDE.

"We know that," I reminded him.

He paid no mind. "I don't think anyone on the block took it, do you?" he asked.

"We checked and it wasn't around."

He wrote—FACT NUMBER TWO: IT'S NOT TO BE SEEN ON THE STREET.

"Since we know everybody around here," he continued, "and we trust them, we can be pretty sure no one here took it."

"Guess so," I agreed.

"Which means it was someone else." He wrote that down.

I nodded.

"Now," he continued, "we get to the hard part. Who came by? Remember, it was Halloween."

It was then that I realized how hopeless it all was. A lot of people came by—all wearing masks and costumes.

"After I got back from trick-or-treating, I'm sure it was still there, cause that's where I always leave it."

"Fine. Who came by after that?"

I could have groaned. "There was Superman, a mummy, four Draculas, Batman, a masked football player, a bunch of witches—one of them one-legged —a masked nurse and a warlock."

"A warlock?" my father asked.

"Sure, a man witch."

My father wrote out the list. "Fine," he said. "Did you recognize any of the people?"

"Most."

"Good. I'll read off the costumes and you give me their real names." He started right off. "Superman."

And I said "Sam."

"First Dracula."

"Jackie."

That's the way it went. When we were done, it turned out there were only a few I didn't know— the one-legged witch, the masked nurse, the warlock, and the mummy.

"About those you know," he went on, "do you think any of them would take your bike?"

"Why should they?"

"Even as a joke?"

"No way," I assured him. "They're my friends."

"Well, that leaves four you don't know. Would Mike know them?"

"He was at the parade."

"Think you could find out who the four were?"

"Suppose so," I said, studying the list. Then I put it down. "Maybe it *was* a ghost or something," I said. "Something magical could've taken the bike. It *was* that special green color. And it was Halloween."

My father smiled. "Go out and get the right questions before you get the wrong answers," he said for the six million and first time. "Nowadays there's no more magic."

I slipped on my Green Lantern ring and went out. I wasn't as sure as he was.

❧ Outside it was still cold, but the sky had turned as blue as anything. Perfect soccer weather. That's why I decided the best place to start was down at the school playing-field.

When I got there a few kids had already set up a game, but instead of playing I sat in the grandstand. From the top level I could see which kids were there. I could also look over where they had left their bikes.

Not every kid in town had a bike. A lot didn't. Some didn't even want them. Some didn't have the money. New bikes are expensive and most kids thought I was a freak for getting an old one. A lot feel that if you don't have a new one, with a banana seat and high-rise handlebars, it's no good.

That's part of what puzzled me. There weren't a lot of kids who would even want my bike. The best thing going for it was its green color, but I never heard anybody say, "Hey, man, that's a cool color," which they would have if they liked it the way I did.

Looking over the bikes I could see right away that mine wasn't one of them. I was glad about that. I'm not sure what I would have done if it had been there. I'm not much of a fighter.

I was still sitting in the stands when Eddie showed up. "You going to play?" he called.

We played about an hour, then the other kids took off, leaving just Eddie and me. I played goalkeeper while he took some shots. After that we sat down. By then I wasn't feeling cold at all.

"What did you get last night?" he asked me.

"Four chocolate lollipops, a bag of popcorn, and a bunch of Milky Ways."

"That all?"

"A lot of other stuff," I told him. "I just don't remember." Actually, my folks only let me stay out till eight, which means I don't get as much as some kids. I didn't feel like saying that to Eddie. "How did you do?" I asked him.

"I got three doughnuts," he began, going on with a huge list of things that made me hungry long before he reached the end.

"Did you get to the parade?" I asked.

"Did you go?" he asked me, instead of answering.

"My folks didn't let me," I told him. "Too late. My brother went though."

Somehow he seemed glad I hadn't gone. "It was great," he let me know. "Too bad you weren't there."

I quickly changed the subject. "Hey," I said, "do you know who that mummy was? With the blood and all?"

"That was Gus," he told me, "and man, is his mother mad."

"Why?"

"He cut up two whole sheets to do that."

"Really?"

"And it took him and his sister an hour to wrap him up. When it was done it was so tight he could hardly walk. Did you see Tony?"

"Count Dracula?"

"He didn't make that costume. He bought it."

"What about the one-legged witch and the warlock?"

"The witch was Peyton. She got some fake blood in her eye and they had to take her to the doctor."

"With her costume on?"

Eddie nodded.

"What about the warlock?"

"How come you're asking all these questions," he said, looking at me.

"Just curious." Then I asked about the warlock again.

"Didn't see him." He asked me if I had seen Micky. "His Tarzan suit was great."

"He put on his own make-up," I told him. "What about the nurse?"

"I don't know her very well. She's new. They call her Muffin."

"Where does she live?" I asked, for I didn't know anything about her.

"Down on Delevan Street."

Except for the identity of the warlock, I had gotten the information I wanted.

Having rested up, we got into another game for a while, then Eddie had to go. Since he had the ball, I started to go back home, trying to keep from stepping on the cracks in the old slate sidewalks.

As I was walking along Franklin Street, where I live, I saw a parked police car. In it was the Police Chief, Chief Byers. In my town there are only two policemen. Byers is in charge, so they called him the Chief. He was talking to someone.

It occurred to me that maybe I should tell him about the bike. He might have seen it somewhere. So I waited till he was finished talking.

"Hi, Chris," he called to me. "How're things?"

"Okay."

"Something on your mind?"

"Well, there is, actually," I said, going up to his car. "Someone stole my bike."

"That's a shame. Where'd you see it last?"

"Outside my house. Last night."

"What's it look like?" he wanted to know, taking up a little pad and writing down my name.

I described it as best I could while he took notes.

"I'll keep it in mind," he said when I'd finished. "Most times I find these stolen bikes in a couple of days." I must have smiled because he added, "That is, when I do find them. Best not to leave things around. The temptation gets to people." Promising to let me know if he learned anything, he drove off.

When I got home it was time for lunch. Saturday lunch at my place is a kind of take-what-you-want business, so Mike and I made sandwiches. We sat around the old oak table next to the kitchen, which is so small there's no place in it to eat. It was then that I told him about my bike.

"That's rotten," he said. Though Mike teases me a lot, I can count on him for help when things get bad.

"It was probably someone who came to the house last night," I told him.

16

"Maybe it was one of your magical super-heroes," he said.

"Don't be funny. Whoever took it was real."

"The warlock too?" he asked.

I told him about my talk with Dad and Eddie. "Did you see any of those people at the parade?" I wanted to know, giving him the list of unknown trick-or-treaters. "The only one I'm not sure of is the warlock."

"Probably real," he said, still teasing me.

Not willing to be put off, I announced I was going around to see those other kids, mostly the one called Muffin, to find out if they knew anything about the bike.

"Want to come with me?" I asked him.

"Sure, I'll protect you against warlocks."

It had gotten colder and gray outside. The houses in town, mostly brick or stone, didn't look very welcoming. Still, we went to Gus's house. But when we knocked on the door his father wouldn't let us come in, or send Gus out. He was being punished for ripping up the sheets.

At Peyton's house we didn't learn anything either. With her getting that fake blood in her eye she hadn't seen much at all. When I asked her about the warlock, she just shrugged.

"See," said Mike. "I told you the warlock was real."

I ignored him.

After that we went down to Delevan Street and tried to find the girl who was called Muffin. It's one of the prettiest streets in town, with lots of trees and no telephone lines in the air. But there were no people around so we decided to go home.

My mother greeted us as soon as we walked in. "You had a call from the Police Chief," she told me. "Maybe something's turned up. He left his number and asked that you call. Don't forget to thank him."

I was so excited I couldn't even dial. My mother had to.

"Can I speak to the Chief, please."

"Chief *Byers,*" my mother coached.

When the Chief got on, I said, "This is Chris."

"Chris, I wanted to tell you that someone did see your bike."

"Where?" I cried, and he could tell I was excited.

"Now hold on, and let me explain," he said carefully. "I was going over some reports and it seems that on Friday night, that's Halloween, Mr. Podler called to report a reckless bike-rider."

"What did he look like?" I asked.

"Mr. Podler wasn't much help. Said it was a

green bike and that the rider had on a strange cape."

"The warlock!" I shouted.

"Warlock?" said the Chief. "I don't know anyone by that name."

"It was someone's costume," I explained.

"Oh. If I catch that kid he'll not only have to give back the bike, but he'll get a good dressing down from me too. According to Mr. Podler he was just walking along when this kid, bike and all, jumped right over him."

"Over him?"

"Well, you know Mr. Podler," said the Chief. "Kids are always bothering him. The point is, at least you know someone took it."

"But who?" I wanted to know.

"That warlock person, or whatever you said."

I hung up, feeling worse than ever. The fact was, as my father would say, Mr. Podler was not the best witness. I knew two things about him. He drank an awful lot. And he was always blaming kids for bothering him.

I told my mother and Mike what the Chief had said. After all his teasing I could see my brother was bothered.

"I bet you're going to blame the warlock for taking your bike," he said.

"Maybe he did," I shot back. "Someday you're going to put your big foot in your mouth."

"Smaller than yours," he retorted.

"You're both being silly," was the way my mother ended that.

∿ I just didn't feel like

doing anything much for the rest of the day. Mike went out with his friends so I stayed up in my room and played, building a neat castle and fighting a war with the plastic knights my mother had gotten for me. I made one Merlin The Magician. That was Saturday.

The next morning, Sunday, we had our usual family breakfast, about the only time the bunch of us get to sit down and take as long as we want. About halfway through my mother said, "I have an idea."

Now when she or my father says that, that's not what they really mean. It's their way of announcing they've decided something.

"Maybe we should get you another bike," she

said. "Mr. Bullen is open on Sundays. I'm sure we could find one."

"What happens if he finds the one he lost?" asked Mike.

"I doubt very much if he will," my father said.

"Mr. Podler said he saw someone with it," I reminded him.

"We all know about Mr. Podler," was my father's answer to that. "Someday I'll tell you about the ghosts he saw in City Hall."

"Don't you want a bike?" my mother asked.

Mike's question was the right one. "What happens if my old one turns up?" I asked.

"We'll worry about that if it happens," suggested my mom. "It's up to you. We can get one if you want."

"If I do get a new one, does that mean I have to stop looking for the old one?" I wanted to know.

"I don't see much point in looking," said my father. "But if you want to, there's no one saying you can't."

"Okay I'll get one."

"I'll go with you," Mike said suddenly. "I need some radio parts."

It was eleven when my mother, Mike with his radio parts box, and I got into the car and drove to

Mr. Bullen's junk yard a little way out of town.

My mother has always had a particular liking for Mr. Bullen, and since she likes junk, it's not hard to see why. The lot is something kind of hard to describe. It has just about everything in the world piled up in heaps, piled up so much that it's hard to find anything. There are some sections, such as shutters, or bathtubs, but aside from those, you just have to go looking and there are more hiding places there than anywhere else.

On the other side of the road is Mr. Bullen's house, with its porch. He sits there on a rocking chair, and when anyone drives up, he comes over.

If anybody looks like a junk dealer, it's Mr. Bullen. He's real small, not much bigger than me. I don't think he has any teeth. He wears old clothes, but then he's old himself. As far as I'm concerned he's at least two hundred years old. Mike says it's more like seventy. He always needs a shave and he doesn't walk so much as he shuffles.

He and my mom get along swell because he doesn't mind her poking around. Then, when she finds something, they bargain. I never got that part straight because my mother once explained it wasn't that Mr. Bullen was expensive, it was just that they both enjoyed bargaining.

We were standing round the car looking over the piles of stuff when Mr. Bullen came over. "Hya," he said. "Looking for something?"

"Greetings, Mr. Bullen," my mother said. "We're looking for a bike for Chris." She nodded to me because I don't think Mr. Bullen knew me from Mike. "His other one was stolen," she added.

"Stolen?" said Mr. Bullen, stopping short, and looking at me. Then he shook his head. "That's too bad. That's what kids are coming to. I've got some over here." And he led the way to a whole bunch of bikes which didn't look too good to me. Most were the newer kind, with fancy designs. One or two even had gears.

"These'll be better than that old green one of yours, anyway," said Mr. Bullen, hauling out a yellow bike with a long banana seat and high-boy handlebars. It hardly looked old at all. "That's a beauty," he said.

I took it from him, more from politeness than anything else. It wasn't bad. It just wasn't my style. Yellow works against the Green Lantern. I looked at my mother.

"Can I try some others?" I asked.

"Help yourself," put in Mr. Bullen. "I'll give you a good deal." Shuffling off, he watched us from his porch rocking chair. Mike went off to look for his radio parts.

After half an hour I narrowed it down to two bikes. Mike, who had come back, was growing impatient. "Come on, Chris, pick one," he urged.

"Pick the one you want," my mother reassured me.

I guess I'm stubborn. My mother says I get it from my father. He says I get it from my mother. Anyway you look at it, I guess I am. The fact is, I didn't want any of them. I wanted my own back.

Then the thought came to me that having a bike would help me track down the other one faster.

"I'll take this one," I announced, putting my hand down on the yellow bike Mr. Bullen had first suggested.

We wheeled it back to the car as Mr. Bullen, who had been watching us, came across the road.

"How much will it be?" my mother wanted to know.

Mr. Bullen chewed on something, looking first at me then at the bike. "You say someone stole your other one."

"That's right," my mother assured him.

"You can have this one for eight-fifty."

That was a fantastic price for a bike so new. But

there it was, my mother and Mr. Bullen had to have their bargaining game.

"Would you take seven?" she said.

He considered. "Eight."

It was worth twenty bucks, easy, but they settled on seven seventy-five.

"I'll ride it home," I told them.

She and Mike got into the car and drove off.

I checked over the bike carefully before getting on it for keeps.

"That's a good bike," said Mr. Bullen, who was standing there watching me.

I was just about to go when I turned to him. "If anyone tries to sell you that old bike of mine, would you let me know?"

"This is a better one," he said strongly. I was afraid I had hurt his feelings.

"I know," I said, "But I liked it. Will you let me know?" I asked him again.

He kept looking at me and then at my new bike. "This is better," he repeated, then went back to his rocking chair.

Halfway home the thought occurred to me that I should go down to Delevan Street to see if I could find the girl named Muffin, the one who'd been the masked nurse.

I kept on going—the bike wasn't bad—and turned onto Delevan Street where I stopped. There were some kids playing about halfway down the block, so I pedaled up to them.

"Any of you know where Muffin lives?" I asked.

"She lives over there," I was told, and they pointed to a wooden house, white, with green shutters and a porch.

When I got closer I looked it over on the chance that my bike was there. I didn't see it.

For a long time I stood there, trying to make up my mind what to do. Muffin was the one person I knew nothing about. Still, that wasn't what made me go to her door. It was the fact that as I was standing there in the middle of the street, I saw someone looking out at me from behind a curtain. It made me jump, but it also made me want to find out about her.

I set my bike up on its kick stand—my old bike had a bad one and was always falling over—and went up to the door and knocked.

The door opened immediately as if I was expected. A girl stood there. Now that I saw her I recognized her as a new kid in town. I remembered her because she had a long braid down her back, just one, which I had never seen on any girl before. She was tall, a little taller than me. Her hair was dark, black even, though her face was very white. It was so pale, it made her mouth seem very red.

"Is Muffin home?" I asked.

"I'm Muffin," she answered me, rather scared I thought.

We sort of stared at each other and I was beginning to feel a little stupid.

"What do you want?" she asked me, speaking so softly I could hardly hear.

"Do you mind my asking what your costume was for Halloween?"

"I had a warlock costume," she answered, her eyes rather big.

❧ When she said hers

was the warlock costume I was surprised as anything. "I thought you were the masked nurse," I blurted out.

"I was," she answered.

"I don't get it. You couldn't have been two different people at once."

"Just a minute," she said, stepping back into her house and going up into the hallway. "I'm going outside," she called.

"What for?" came a voice in reply.

"Just want to," was Muffin's answer.

"Be back in fifteen minutes," came an order.

Shutting the door firmly behind her, Muffin sat down on the edge of the porch steps, not even bothering to look at me. I couldn't figure her out at all.

"I'll explain," she said, "if you tell me why you're asking."

I wasn't certain how much information to give her. For all I knew she was the one who had taken the bike.

"Just curious," I tried. "Some kids came to my place Friday night trick-or-treating, and I wanted to know who they were."

"What makes you think I went to your house?" she asked, which made me feel as though she knew I wasn't telling the whole truth.

"Do you know Eddie?"

"No."

"He's in the fourth grade, Mr. Ciccarelli's class. I'm in that class too. When I asked him who the masked nurse was, he said it was you. But you said you were the warlock?"

"I was the nurse," she said firmly. "Did a warlock come to your house?"

"Sure did."

"What did he look like?"

"Well," I told her, "he had a cape, sort of checked, a three-cornered hat, and a weird face. I guess it was a rubber mask."

"That's it, all right," she said, and for a second I thought she gasped.

"What's it?" I asked.

"My costume."

"You've mixed me all up," I complained. "A minute ago you said you were the nurse."

"I was."

"Forget it," I said, starting to go over to my bike. But I really didn't want to go. "Are you sure you can't explain it to me?" I asked. Looking at her, it suddenly occurred to me that she was about to cry. I said about to. She never did. "What's the matter?" I asked in a nicer way.

"That warlock costume was *mine!*" she said, almost fiercely. "Somebody stole it."

"Stole it!" I cried. "From you?" She nodded. "When?"

"Friday afternoon."

I sat back on the seat of my bike. "Who would do that?"

She shook her head. "I haven't made too many friends yet," she said, sadly, I thought.

"Someone just stole it?" I asked again. I had never heard of someone stealing a costume before.

"I made the whole thing myself," she said. "Except for the mask. Nobody helped me. Then I spilled milk on it. I washed it, and hung it out to dry right here. I never thought anyone would steal it. But when I came out for it, it was gone."

"Someone came to my house in that costume," I told her.

"It wasn't me. I had to think up another one. My aunt suggested a nurse." She made a face that showed she didn't think much of the idea. "It was all right, but I'd spent a lot of time on the other one."

"It *was* good," I told her. "It looked real. The best costume I saw." I was trying to make her feel better.

"How come you're so interested?" she asked.

Before I answered I had to think. I was getting more confused about the whole thing. Finally I said, "Do you mind if I ask you something?"

"Depends what."

"You won't get sore?"

"Ask me and you'll see."

"Did you steal my bike?"

Instead of getting mad she looked at me crossly.

"Do you think I did?" she asked.

Right away I felt sorry that I had said it. "No, I guess not."

"Just because I'm new around here?" she demanded, her voice getting hard.

"No, not really," I explained quickly. "I knew all the other kids and they wouldn't have done it. You're the only one I didn't know. So I just thought I should find out." Then, without her even asking, I told her everything that had happened, sort of as an apology. When I finished, I added, "By the way, my name is Chris."

"My name is Muffin."

"I never heard that name before."

"That's not my real name. It's Maureen," she said, letting me know she didn't like that one much.

"Seems to me," I said, trying to talk it out, "that someone stole your costume, then came over to my place to steal my bike."

"On purpose?" she asked, looking at me.

"It does sound crazy," I admitted.

"Then," she suggested, "if we find who took your bike, we can find who took my costume."

An idea came to me. "Did you go trick-or-treating alone?" I asked her. She nodded. I was impressed. "When I go out," I told her, "my father usually goes with me. Not exactly with me, but near. I'd rather he didn't, but I feel better that he does."

"I live with my aunt," she said.

"What happened to your parents?"

"They're not around," she replied, matter-of-factly.

I didn't know what to say. I wanted to ask her where they were. Then I wanted to say I was sorry, but that didn't seem good either.

"What about the parade? Did you go there?"

She shook her head no.

I thought for a moment. "I'll tell you what," I finally said, "I really want to find that bike of mine. You want your costume back?"

She didn't say yes or no.

"We could work as a team," I urged. "My father is always saying that when you have an idea you have to test it out on other people, cause when you talk to yourself nobody is listening."

"He said that?"

"That's the way he talks. What about it?"

"How would we do it?" she asked, still not giving me any kind of answer.

"Some kid took our things," I insisted. "If he wore your costume, he can't be too big. If he's not too big, he has to come from around here. He didn't drive a car."

"It could be a small grownup," she suggested.

"The point is," I went on, "if he's around here we can find him, right?"

"You have another bike, don't you?"

"I'd rather have the old one," I told her.

"I'll do it," she finally said.

From the house her aunt called. Muffin made a face. Quickly, we talked about different ways to go about looking for the things. When her aunt called a second time we were only able to agree to meet after school the next day.

By then it was time for me to go home anyway. Sunday is ice-cream day at my house. I also wanted to tell everybody what I had found out.

But as soon as I walked into the house my brother said, "Find the warlock?"

Right then I decided not to tell him what I had learned. Muffin and I would do it all on our own.

∾ After school I met

Muffin on the playground. She was sitting in the old grandstand wrapped up in the strangest coat I had ever seen. When I first saw it I thought it was a checkerboard, its design was so funny. But when I came up close I could see it was made up of pictures of fluttering wings. No two ways about it, she wasn't like anybody else I knew.

I wasn't sure if I should go over to her right away or play soccer. But she looked sort of lonely up there, and I had promised to meet her, so I went to the bottom of the seats and called up to her.

"Hi."

She looked down at me. Peeping out from that coat, which was a little big for her, she looked like a squirrel in a tree hole.

"That's quite a coat," I said.

"It's warm," she answered.

I looked over to where the other kids were getting ready to play soccer, then back to her. "Want to play?"

She looked unsure.

"You can be on my team," I told her. "Only I don't think you should wear that coat." She looked at me with a funny tilt to her chin. I wasn't sure, but I thought it meant, "I'm not that stupid."

The coat must have weighed a ton. Once it came off, she came down the steps fast and started to run toward the game. She was a good runner.

When we got to the others I introduced her.

"This is Muffin. She's on my team." That done, we got lined up pretty quickly and the game got going. I could tell at first that the guys weren't too sure about letting her play, but since I brought her and they knew I was good, they didn't say anything.

I suppose if it had been on television she would have been fantastic and scored fifteen goals. It wasn't television, and she was lousy. All the same, she didn't give up. She kept right on getting in on everything, even where it was muddy, her long braid flying behind her. I think I liked her better for that than if she had been fantastic. When the others saw she wasn't going to cop out on anything they just played right along and we had a good game for at least an hour.

"I wasn't very good, was I?" she asked me as we walked back to the seats to get her stuff.

"You were all right," I said, not wanting to tell how bad she was.

"Well, I never played before."

"Really?" I said, stopping.

"Couldn't you tell?" she asked, with that look again.

"I guess not." I didn't say anything else, but I thought she was even better for never having played before and not giving up on anything.

As we walked off the field she got into that weird coat of hers. "Let's go over to my place," I suggested. "We can get something to eat."

"I'm supposed to go home," she told me.

Right then Eddie called from across the field.

"What?" I yelled back.

"Want to play?"

"That's Eddie," I explained to Muffin. "My best friend."

"Want to?" Eddie yelled again.

"I'll go to your house," said Muffin.

"I'm going home," I called to Eddie. He looked at us for a minute and then joined in a game.

When we got to my house Mike was out in the back yard playing with friends. My mother was home though, reading a newspaper.

"Greetings," she said. Nobody else's mother ever says that, but my mother always does.

"This is Muffin," I announced. "This is my mother. Can we have something to eat?" I asked.

"You can have apples," was all that was offered. I went into the kitchen to get a couple. When I came back my mother was looking over that coat of Muffin's.

"Where did you get it?" she was asking Muffin.

"Why?" Muffin wanted to know.

"It looks like it was made in Eastern Europe," explained my mother. I should say that my mother, who's a weaver, always examines people's clothing, telling them more than they ever want to know. I find it embarrassing.

"Do you mind if I look at it closer," my mother went on. She's a real cloth freak.

I think Muffin did mind but there wasn't much she could do about it. My mother helped her off with the coat and then went out of the room to look at it under bright light. Muffin and I sat down at the table to eat. All of a sudden she sort of spat out the piece she was eating.

"Look!" she cried in a sort of whisper. She was pointing at the newspaper my mother had been reading. It was the local one—comes out once a week.

There, on the front page, was a picture of the warlock. Next to him was the Mayor giving the warlock a prize trophy cup. Underneath the picture was a caption which read—

Mayor Rinaldi gives award for best costume
at Halloween Parade to warlock.
Story and pictures on page 6.

On page six was the story about the Halloween parade, with a list of kids who marched and their costumes. We turned back to the front page and stared at the picture.

"That's him all right," I said, bending closer to see if I could see any better.

"Do you recognize him at all?" Muffin asked me.

"He could be anyone," I replied.

"Anyone shorter than the Mayor."

"Yeah, he only comes up to his shoulders," I agreed. "But I can't see anything else about him."

My mother came back into the room. "This is certainly interesting," she announced. For a moment I thought she was into what we were talking about, but she wasn't. She was still going on about Muffin's coat.

"I never saw anything quite like it before," she said. "I can't even figure out how it was done. Don't you have any idea where it came from?" she questioned Muffin.

"Nope," said Muffin who didn't seem to care one way or the other. She kept her eyes on the picture of the warlock.

"Do you mind if I take it upstairs?" asked my mother. "I have a book I want to check it with."

"No, I don't mind," said Muffin. Lugging the coat, my mother went up.

"What about the list?" Muffin suddenly said.

"What about it?"

"There was that list of all the kids who were there and their costumes. It should say who the warlock was."

That was a great idea so I quickly turned to the list. I read it through once, then twice. There must have been seventy or eighty names. "No warlock listed," I announced.

She checked for herself. "Can you tell anything?" she wanted to know.

I went over it a couple of more times, trying to think about it carefully. There *was* something about it that got to me, but I couldn't figure it out. I read it through for the sixth time.

"What are you thinking?" she asked me.

Just then my mother came down with the coat.

"I can't find out much," she said, looking more baffled than ever. "And I don't see how it was done that way. I made a sketch of it. It's really fascinating. Who gave it to you?"

After a moment she said, "My mother."

"Do you know where she got it?"

"She never told me," said Muffin, and it occurred to me that she really didn't want to talk about it.

"Could you ask her? I'm really curious."

Muffin shrugged. "I guess so."

"Eddie!" I shouted.

"What about Eddie?" my mother said.

"He's not on the list!"

"What list? What in heaven's name are you talking about?"

But Muffin knew.

"He said he went to the parade," I said. "But he's not listed."

❧ "I'm sure," I said as we sat out on the front steps thinking about what to do next, "that Eddie told me he went to the parade."

"He wasn't on the list," she said, as if I needed reminding.

"Do you know anything about Eddie?" I asked her. She shook her head. "He's a pretty nice guy. Sort of shy, and he doesn't like girls. A little bigger than me, but not any stronger. His parents and my parents are friends. And he's my best friend."

"Do you think he would have taken your bike as a joke?" she wanted to know.

"I never would have thought so. But then, when he told me he was in the parade, I believed that too."

"I think," she said firmly, "we should investigate him."

I didn't like the way that sounded. "Why not just ask him," I said.

"He lied once, didn't he?"

"That's not fair," I insisted. "I just think he didn't tell the truth. I don't always. Do you?" She didn't answer. "Maybe there are reasons," I went on. "Get the right questions before you get the wrong answers," I put in, and the way I said it made me feel funny, because it sounded just like my father talking to me.

"Where does Eddie live?" Muffin asked.

"Fleecy Dale Road, about two miles out of town. You can get there by bike. I do a lot."

"I don't have a bike."

"Do you know how to ride?" I said, acting like I had been riding all my life.

"I used to have one."

"What happened to it?"

Instead of answering she shrugged. She didn't seem to like to talk much about herself.

"Would you want one?" I said.

"I guess so."

"Would your folks get you one?"

"My aunt," she corrected me.

"Well, would she?"

"It would cost too much."

I pointed toward my new bike. "Guess how much I paid for it?"

"Thirty dollars."

"Seven dollars and seventy-five cents," I said.

"Where?"

I told her about Bullen's. She had never heard of the place. I explained how he had a lot of cheap bikes. "Look," I said, "do you get an allowance?"

"Sometimes," she said evasively.

That didn't seem too helpful, but by then I had an idea. "If we really are going to investigate all this, you *have* to have a bike. Do you have any money of your own saved up?"

She thought for a bit. "About four dollars, I think."

"Wait here," I told her. I ran into my house and up to my room where my bank was. Pulling the bottom plug out, pennies, dimes, quarters, and nickles dropped all over the floor. I put them into piles and added them up. It came to two dollars and sixty-three cents.

I got a bag from the kitchen and threw the coins in, then I ran outside to where Muffin was waiting.

"Look," I cried. "I've got almost three bucks. You said you had four. That's seven. We could go up to Bullen's and get you a bike."

"It's not enough," she worried.

"I can bargain with him."

By then we were so excited that we went back to her place with me giving her a ride, which wasn't easy, because, like I said, she's slightly bigger than me. In fact, on the way we passed Mrs. Lebor, the school counselor, and when I tried to wave we almost fell.

I waited outside while Muffin got her money. As it turned out she had a little more than she thought, so it came to almost eight bucks.

"Let's go," I urged.

"I can't," she whispered. "My aunt says no."

I didn't like that aunt of hers. Obviously she was a real zero. But there was nothing to do but agree to meet after school the next day and get the bike. I gave her the money to keep. We also agreed not to talk to Eddie about our suspicions.

As it turned out, avoiding Eddie was no problem. He wasn't in school that day. Mr. Ciccarelli said something about his having a cold. A lot of kids were out with colds so it probably wasn't too serious.

After school I didn't see Muffin around, so I waited. When she finally came out, she was looking kind of angry.

"What's the matter?" I asked her.

"Teachers are so nosey," was all she would say in her most angry voice.

She had the money bag and I had my bike so we went right to Bullen's. On the way I asked if her aunt said it was okay.

"I didn't ask."

"Why?"

"If I did she'd say 'no.'"

We pulled up to Mr. Bullen's lot and looked it over. He was sitting on his rocking chair, but he didn't do anything. Only when we started to go into the lot did he get up and hurry across.

"Hya. Looking for something?"

"Hello Mr. Bullen. Remember me? I'm Chris."

"Your bike okay?" he wanted to know.

"It's fine," I told him. I kept having the feeling that he was insulted that I had taken the green one and that he wanted me to admit that my new one was better.

Sure enough he said, "That one's better than your old one, isn't it?"

I didn't really want to talk about it. "It's pretty good," I told him. "Mr. Bullen, this is my friend, Muffin."

He didn't seem very interested. "How do," he said in his nodding way.

"She wants a bike too," I explained. "Do you have any good ones like the one I got? We've got seven dollars and ninety-four cents."

He shook his head. "You can't get much with that kind of money."

"My bike cost only seven seventy-five," I reminded him.

"That was special. Your other one got lost."

"Stolen," Muffin said suddenly.

Mr. Bullen turned to look at her a bit more closely but didn't say anything. "Well, let's see what we have," and he led the way in and around the junk heaps till we came to where the bikes were.

He looked them over then pulled one out from behind a door. It didn't look like much. Once it must have been silver, but it had gotten rusty. The seat was cockeyed, and there seemed to be a few busted things.

"You can have it for eight," he said to Muffin who was examining the bike closely.

"Does it work?" I asked Mr. Bullen.

He shrugged.

Muffin, bending over the bike, was checking out the parts that seemed broken, rubbing her hands over some of the rusty spots and the places where it needed repairs. "It's not too bad," she said. "I can fix it up."

I really didn't think she was right about that, but I looked again. In fact, to my surprise, on second look it *was* somewhat better, as if some rust had gone. "Doesn't look too bad," I had to admit.

"How much did you say it was?" Muffin asked Mr. Bullen.

Mr. Bullen pulled at his ear. "Tell you what, if you give me that coat, you can have the bike."

I think he was only kidding, but I was angry anyway. "That coat's worth more than eight bucks," I said.

"Oh?" he answered. "What makes you think so?"

I couldn't tell if he was just kidding around or not. "My mother said so," I told him. "She's trying to figure out where it's from."

Mr. Bullen acted as if he didn't care. "Eight bucks," he said, nodding toward the bike.

It was time for *me* to bargain. "Seven-seventy," I said back.

"Seven ninety-nine," he said.

"Seven ninety-three," was my final offer.

He thought a minute. "Okay," he said, holding out his hand. Muffin gave him the money and took the penny change.

As we started to go out of the lot, Muffin, wheeling the new bike, whispered to me. "Ask him about Eddie?"

"What about?" I said, puzzled.

"Ask him if he knows him."

I couldn't figure that one out, but as Muffin went ahead I waited for Mr. Bullen to catch up with me. "Mr. Bullen, do you know Eddie?"

"Who's Eddie?"

"He's a friend of mine." As I said that I knew why Muffin wanted to know. "Maybe," I said to Mr. Bullen, "maybe he was the one who took my bike."

"What's he look like?"

I described him as best I could.

"Where does he live?" he asked me, and I told him that too. "You think he took your bike?"

I felt bad, blaming Eddie that way. "I don't know for sure."

"No, I don't know him at all."

Muffin was waiting for me by the entrance to the junk yard.

"Did he know him?" she asked me.

"Nope."

"Is your bike all right?" I called out to her as we were going down the road.

"Perfect," she called back.

I took a quick look at it. Now that we were out from under the shadows, there didn't seem to be hardly any rust or bad spots on it. She was right. It was a good deal after all. I prided myself on being a good bargainer.

❧ The next couple of days it was raining, so we couldn't very well go out to Eddie's. He wasn't in school either, cause his cold had turned into the flu. That made it impossible for me to talk to him. And I did want to talk. His being a best friend, I felt sort of funny even thinking that he had taken my bike or Muffin's costume. I was even a little annoyed that Muffin thought he was guilty. After all, she was only a new friend.

But friend she was. Those two afternoons she came over to my place and played. We had a good time. She never asked me to go over to her house, but some kids are like that. For all I knew it was her aunt who didn't want people around. In fact, her aunt called my mother—my father answered but she wouldn't speak to him—to ask about the bike-buying bit. My mother said it was fine with her. She told me that Muffin's aunt made a thing about Muffin having a friend who was a boy. Like I said, zero.

On Friday the weather was clear. I had wanted to say something to Muffin about my feelings about Eddie, but I never did. And right after school we took off.

It's only two miles to Eddie's, through some of the prettiest places around, real forest. The road's kind of narrow, sort of cut out from the side of a hill. On the other side of the road, down a gully, is a stream. In the fall it isn't much to look at. During the spring, when the snow melts and a lot of rain comes, it's wild. During the summer it's just nice.

The best part of the stream is only a quarter of a mile from Eddie's house, near the bridge, where the water is damned up. I stopped to show it to Muffin.

From the bridge you can look right down into the pool of water. There are tall trees growing up on two sides of it, like walls. Their reflection on the water makes it seem like an iron gate has been laid across. On the third side—the stream takes a bend there—is a cliff of solid rock which runs right down into the water. It's cold water, but during the summer it's a fantastic place to swim. You can jump off the bridge, cannon balling to make a great splash.

Best of all is its color, green—green as deep down as you can see, and you can't even see the bottom. Eddie's mother said it was just green algae. I like to think it's a special water passage to the Land of Oz. Or maybe it's Green Kryptonite (which makes Superman weak) down there. As I've said before, I like green.

I pointed all this out to Muffin who was really impressed with the place.

"How far down does it go?" she asked me.

"Some kids say a thousand feet," I told her. She was even more impressed. "My father says it's only twelve. I've never gone all the way down. You have to be a great swimmer. When I'm older I will. Can you swim?"

"A little," she answered.

"I swim on that side," I said pointing upstream. "It's not deep there at all, and even has a sandy bottom. When it's a hot day this is a great place."

She looked at it carefully and we even talked about its magic, but soon she suggested we get to Eddie's.

Eddie's house is one of the oldest in the area, a stone house which I think had been built when George Washington was around. So it was really ancient. It's up above the road, mostly covered with ivy and trees. It's not as if you could miss it. But when it's dark, the brown stone and all those growing things moving in the wind—well, it is kind of strange. Enough so you might want to miss it.

To get to his house you have to leave your bike down by the road and climb up a flight of steep steps which in the dark always makes me think of castles, or falling—not that I ever did fall.

When we got to the house we parked our bikes, and then I almost quit. Eddie's parents and my parents are friends. His mother takes pictures and his father teaches at my father's school. And Mike sometimes plays with Eddie's older brothers. So I was really bothered about even thinking he did what I thought he did.

"Don't you think we should look around first?" I said.

"What for?"

"The bike."

"I think we should just ask him."

"If you don't know him how come you don't like him?" I said hotly. I felt she was being unfair. She must have seen that I was angry, because she didn't say anything.

Not even looking to see if she was following, I went right up and knocked. Eddie's mother opened the door.

"Hi, Chris."

"Eddie all right?" I asked her.

"Oh, sure," she said. I could tell she was pleased that I'd come to ask, which made me feel worse. "We just thought it'd be better to get the flu all done with," she explained.

"Can I speak to him?"

"Sure. He's up in his room."

"This is Muffin," I said.

"Hello, Muffin. Come on in."

I'd been to Eddie's house so many times I knew where to go. We found Eddie in his room lying on his stomach reading comic books. He hardly looked up at us when we walked in, so we sat down on the bench by the window and just watched him read.

"You feeling better?" I finally asked.

"Sure. I miss anything in school?"

"We started a new project," I told him.

"What about?"

"Geography."

With all that he kept right on reading. For a moment no one said anything. Muffin sort of kicked me.

"Hey, Eddie . . ."

"What?"

"Can I ask you something?"

"Depends what."

"Did you really go to the Halloween parade?" That did it. Though he didn't move I could tell he stopped reading the comic.

"What do you want to know for?" he said.

"Well, you said you did, but when I looked in the newspaper your name wasn't on the list."

"So what?" I could see his hand was shaking.

"Well, how come?" I repeated.

All at once Eddie swung around and sat up, staring at me and Muffin.

"How come you brought her?" he demanded. "Is she your girl friend or something? Bet it was her idea to check lists."

Eddie never has anything good to say about girls so I wasn't going into that. "I just wanted to know," I said. "Were you or weren't you there?"

"I was there," he said sarcastically.

"Then how come you weren't on the parade list?"

Eddie got very red in the face. "What's it to you?" he said, and he was so angry I saw tears start, but only start.

"What costume did you have on?"

"If you must know," he said scornfully, "it was my Batman suit. Just because your parents didn't let you go to the parade, baby, that doesn't mean I couldn't."

"I just wanted to know."

"Why?"

"Do you have any proof that you were there?" said Muffin.

"What's it to you?" He really didn't like her.

"Did you have my warlock costume on?" she finally asked.

"Warlock?" He was amazed. "Are you kidding?"

"Then how come," I said, "you weren't listed?"

"That's none of your business," he repeated.

"*Do* you have proof?" repeated Muffin, who was, I thought, being a little hard on him.

He thought for a moment. "Course I do. My mother took some pictures of me at the parade."

"If you were. at the parade why didn't you march?" I wanted to know.

He just wasn't going to say.

"Let's see the pictures," said Muffin.

"Listen, stupid," he said in a really angry voice, "she hasn't developed them yet. That shows how much you know. I wish you two would get out."

"I'll believe you when I see those pictures," said Muffin as she walked out of the room.

I felt awful, all mixed up. "I just want my bike back," I said, but I don't even know if he heard me.

"You can go now too," he said in his best sarcastic voice. "Your girl friend's gone."

As we passed over the bridge by the swimming hole on our way back to town, Muffin turned to ask me, "Does Eddie swim?"

"Oh, sure. He's the best swimmer I know. Why?" She didn't answer.

✺ It was getting dark,

and with all that forest crowding in on us, I was anxious to get home. In town we split up with no more than a "See ya."

Actually, I was upset, really upset. We had all but accused my best friend of doing something wrong, taking my bike for one, and I felt awful about it. But I had to admit he had told me something that wasn't true, and he wasn't giving much in the way of an explanation. He even acted guilty. Still, it just didn't seem right to me, any of it. When you like someone, love them even, it's hard to tell them they're wrong. Except your parents, that is. With them it's easy.

When I got home I went right to my room, climbed up on my bunk bed, and just lay there thinking about things. For a long time I just stared at the wooden ceiling, seeing if any new cracks had opened up.

What worried me most of all was this—what if Eddie *did* take my bike and Muffin's costume? What if he couldn't prove he really was at that parade? Then what was I to do? I kept thinking that the Police Chief would call me up and say, "Hello, Chris. Did you ever find out who stole your bike?" What was I going to say then?

The trouble with having best friends is that no matter what, you like them too much to hate them.

I was lying there, thinking about all that, when I heard my mother call up for me. I ignored her the first few times, but about the fourth time she got angry. I yelled back, "I'm coming." About five minutes later she came up to my room.

"Didn't you hear me?" she wanted to know.

"I'm coming," I said, flat on my back.

"Slowly."

"What is it?" I asked her. I'm not usually rude, but I really felt rotten.

"I need to speak to you."

When in doubt blame your brother. "Mike did it," I said automatically.

My mother laughed. "You can just stay up there while I sit here," she said, taking my desk chair. Her voice sounded like it was something important, so I just listened.

"Where did you go this afternoon?" was her first question.

Right away I began to feel guilty. Eddie's mother must have called.

"I went to Eddie's house."

"Is he feeling all right?" she asked, trying to make me feel better.

"What is it?" I demanded.

But she went on *her* way. "Did you go alone?"

"With Muffin. Why?"

"She seems like a nice girl," my mother said, but it was really a question she was asking.

"She's all right," I answered.

"Do you know much about her?"

I don't think my mother had ever asked me that about any of my friends before. She was making me nervous.

"I told you. She's all right. Why do you want to know?"

She sort of sighed. "I had a call from Mrs. Lebor this afternoon," she explained.

That really mixed me up. I couldn't figure out why the school counselor would call. "How come?" I wanted to know.

"I guess she's noticed that you've become friends with Muffin, so she just thought it would be good for you, or me really, to know something about her."

I sat up. "I can't see what business it is of hers!"

My mother was not going to get angry in return. "That's what I thought at first. I was even going to say that to her, but she said it to me first, even apologized for doing it."

"She did it anyway," I pointed out.

"I think she had a good reason."

"Like what?"

"Sometimes," my mother said in a soft voice, "it's good to know about people. It helps you understand them better, even to help them. Have you ever spoken to her about who she is, her parents, or things like that?"

I had of course, but she hadn't wanted to talk about it. I said nothing.

"You do know," she continued, "don't you, that she isn't living with her parents."

"Her aunt," I said, showing her I wasn't that dumb.

"Do you know why?"

"Will you please tell me!" I cried out. "I don't understand what you're saying!"

"I don't think you should talk to her about what I'm going to tell you. I'm letting you know because I think it's important for you to understand. You're old enough to deal with complicated things."

If she was trying to make me feel better it wasn't working.

"About two months ago," my mother began, "it seems Muffin's mother . . . well, she left."

"What about it?" I said impatiently.

"Just try to listen to me, honey. Her father, who was a postman, was suddenly left alone with Muffin. As I understand it, he was very surprised about her mother's leaving. He was upset, naturally. He couldn't accept the idea that Muffin's mother didn't love him any more."

"Did he love her?"

"I don't know," my mother said quietly. "I hope

so. Perhaps not. He was certainly unhappy. But his wife was upset too, maybe more so. And Muffin was very upset. Now, when people get upset they sometimes aren't willing to accept simple truth. They find other reasons. Sometimes they even invent them. Muffin is like that."

"What does she think it was?"

"Apparently, magic."

"Magic!" It was like I was hit on the head.

"So I understand."

"Why did she think it was magic?" I wanted to know.

"Mrs. Lebor doesn't know. Children have a way of inventing things," she said, smiling at me.

"What happened then?"

"After a couple of weeks her father decided he had to find his wife, and I suppose try to work things out. The point is, he sent Muffin to his sister's house while he went off."

"Where?"

"I'm afraid no one knows," said my mother. "He wasn't supposed to be away so long. But when he was, her aunt had to put her in school here. The point is, Muffin claims it was magic that took them away and magic that keeps them gone."

"He just disappeared? Left her?"

"I know it sounds awful. Remember, I don't know the whole story. Still, in a sense that's what's happened. Fortunately, Muffin's aunt has been able to look after her. And the father, at least, should come back soon.

"According to Mrs. Lebor, Muffin really believes in all this magic. And I gather she doesn't have too many friends. Mrs. Lebor thought other children were frightened of her."

"Why?"

"Not many people take magic seriously the way you do," she said. "Mrs. Lebor is really glad you've become friends. She feels you're a good person for her to be with. She thinks highly of you, 'very down-to-earth and sensible,' she said." My mother smiled. "Are you?"

"I don't know," I answered, not even thinking about that.

My mother stood up. "I just thought you should know. It's sort of sad, but that's the way it is. Has she ever mentioned any of this to you?"

I was flat out on my bed again. "Nope."

My mother came over to my bed, her eyes level with mine. "Have I gotten you upset?"

"No," I lied.

"Good. She seems like a nice person. Sometime,

Chris, if you want her to come for supper, or sleep over, that will be fine. Just let us know. I think I could get her aunt to agree." For a minute she stood there, studying me.

"When people are upset, or mixed up," she said, "it's good for them to see a family that's happy like ours."

"Are we happy?"

"Don't you think so?"

"Sometimes you have arguments with Dad."

"We don't always agree because we're different people. And we have strong feelings. But we usually manage to work it out. Haven't you ever gotten mad at Eddie?"

"I guess so," I admitted.

"Well?" she questioned, as if the answer was obvious. She gave a toss to my hair and started to go out of the room.

"Mom!" I called.

She stopped.

"Do you believe in any of that magic?"

"Of course not. There's no such thing as magic any more."

"That's just what Dad said. I thought you were different."

She laughed. "I'm glad you're her friend. She

seems very nice. Supper will be ready soon. I'm making something Chinese. Wash your hands." With that she left the room.

✌ I could hardly sit

through dinner I was thinking so hard. I just ate, didn't talk much. My mother must have said something to my father about our talk, because he didn't ask me how things were at school, or if I had read any good comics lately, or any of those questions he always asks. Mike did most of the talking, about a radio club he wanted to set up. Radio. Big deal.

It was my turn to clear the table which I did. Then I did my homework. After that I listened to records of the Green Hornet and Superman which my father had gotten for me. They were the old radio programs he used to listen to when he was my age.

I went up to bed about eight, took a shower, and got into bed. Usually, when I'm in bed I read for a while—Oz books—or draw comics, but that time I just wanted to think about all the things that were in my head. While I was doing that I remembered my father's way of writing down everything.

I got a piece of paper, a pencil, and a book to lean on, then wrote down just the way he had:

WHO STOLE THE BIKE?

1. The bike was stolen from my house on Halloween night.
2. It was stolen after I got back from trick- or-treating.
3. That same day, Muffin's warlock costume was stolen.
4. Somebody wearing that warlock costume came to my house.
5. Eddie said he went to the Halloween parade, but gave no proof.
6. He wasn't on the parade list.
7. The warlock was at the parade and even won the award for the best costume.
8. The warlock must not have told anybody who he was because it was a stolen suit.
9. Mr. Podler told the Police Chief that someone (who looked just like the warlock) rode a bike (just like mine) right *over* him.
10. Muffin's mother disappeared.
11. Muffin's father disappeared.

I read and reread that list twenty times. It all seemed very strange, hard to believe that it was all

connected to my lost bike, but I certainly had a
ing it was.

I tried to remember everything that had happened
to see if I had left anything out. I kept thinking that
I had forgotten a few things that were part of the
whole problem. But no matter how hard I tried none
of it came together, even though I did try to do what
my father had said, about getting the right questions
before you got the wrong answers.

Hardest of all to figure out was the idea that my
bike had something to do with Muffin's parents. I
was sure Muffin thought that, even though she
hadn't said anything about it. I wondered if I should
ask her. After all, *I* wasn't so sure there was no more
magic.

I was thinking about that for a long time when I
suddenly remembered one of the things I had left
out—Muffin's new bike.

What I remembered was this: When we first
went up to Mr. Bullen's, looking for a bike for her,
the one she had picked out wasn't much. I remembered how rusty it looked, no good at all. Then, she
had put her hands on the bad parts. The next time I
looked at the bike it wasn't so rusty anymore! It had
been like . . . magic!

That proved to me like anything that all the

facts, from my own special green bike to what had happened to Muffin's parents *were* tied up together. They just had to be.

I lay there thinking and thinking about it until all that thinking made me feel hungry. I decided to get up and get something to eat. My folks don't mind if I eat an apple after I've brushed my teeth.

So I got up and went downstairs. Nobody else was around. I got out an apple, then went into the living room to sit down in our big chair. I still had all that magical stuff going through my mind.

The living room's not a big room, and it's kind of cold cause it has a stone floor and brick walls. I wrapped the couch blanket that my mother had made around me to keep from shivering. I got cozy soon.

Sitting there, I looked out the window which was just across from the chair. It's a pretty big window and looks out on our backyard. The yard was really lit up because the moon, which was just rising and kind of yellowy, was big, big as a soccer ball. It was beautiful that way. I could see the places where the spacemen landed, it was that clear and bright.

I was just sitting there, looking at the moon, feeling warm and sleepy when I saw something going through the sky.

Flying right across the moon was a *bicycle!* My bike! I could see it was green. And someone was riding it, like a witch on a broom. The person was all hunched over, not very big, with a long black-and-white checked cape flowing out behind. And the warlock—for that's who it was—had a three-cornered cap on, and from under that cap hung a scarf, or maybe even a long braid. There was no question about it. That's exactly what I saw.

Carefully, I watched as the warlock crossed the moon, pedaling hard, like going uphill. But it *was* the warlock and it was my bike.

When I woke the next morning I was still sitting in the chair downstairs. I wasn't sleepy at all. I remembered everything I had seen, exactly.

When my father came down he was surprised to see me there.

"Hey," he reminded me, "no breakfast without getting dressed. And wake Mike, will you. I'll make some eggs."

I got dressed, and while my father read the paper I ate my breakfast and tried to make up my mind whether to talk to him about what I had seen or not. I wasn't sure what he would say.

"Any plans for today?" he asked me, while he was up getting a second cup of coffee.

67

"I'm not sure yet," I told him.

He gave me a look. "You sleep in that chair all night?" I didn't give him an answer.

All the same, he said, "Your mother told me about Muffin and your talk. Is that what you're thinking about?"

"Sort of," I admitted.

"Want to talk about it?"

If Mike had been there I wouldn't have said anything. But he always took a long time to come down. So I made up my mind. "It's not about that," I said in a way which made him turn around. "I do need to talk to you about something important."

"Sure. Go right ahead." He put his paper off to one side and looked straight at me.

"Well," I started, not sure how to begin, "it's partly about Muffin, partly not. Mostly it's about my bike."

"I thought you'd given up on that."

"I saw it," I let him know.

"Where?"

Right off, I told him what I had seen the night before, the whole thing, just as it happened. I didn't tell him about the stuff before, about Eddie, or Muffin's magic, just about my seeing the bike. He listened, without saying anything.

When I was done he picked up his coffee, took

a drink, swallowed, put the cup down, and said, casual-like, "Sounds to me like you fell asleep in that chair and had a dream."

"You're wrong. I saw it."

He didn't say anything to that. I think he was a bit puzzled but didn't want to admit that. So he tried another way. "I know it would be exciting if it were true. But it looks to me like you had all this magic stuff in your mind, and there you are, you dreamed it. It happens to me sometimes. Sometimes I dream books. Dreams are funny things. They can be so real you believe them."

"I'm not lying."

"Now, Chris, I didn't say you were. I said you had a fantastic dream and you've mixed it up with what's really happened."

I shook my head.

He took on his thoughtful look. "Maybe whether it's a dream or not doesn't matter. What are you going to do about it?"

As soon as he said that I knew it had been a mistake to have even told him about what I had seen. He just didn't believe in the same things I did. So I lied to him. Right then and there I lied.

"Nothing," I answered as easy as I could make it. "Maybe you're right. I guess I was thinking too much about it. Did you ever have dreams like that?"

He fell for it. He began to talk about dreams he had had and I was off the hook.

Breakfast done, dishes washed, bed made, I got out of the house fast. There was plenty I had to do.

❦ As soon as I saw that my father wasn't going to believe what I told him, I decided it would be up to me to work things out by myself. I knew what I had seen. Also, I knew a lot of facts he didn't. "Get the questions right before you get the answers wrong," he had told me so many times. Well, I had the right questions. It was time to see the Mayor.

One of the nice things about my town, at least my folks say so, is that the mayor and all those kinds of people are around. The Mayor, for example, runs a shoe store. That's where we go to get our sneakers. I like to go there, because when we do usually there's something there for kids—balloons, or something like that. If you ask me, Mr. Rinaldi, that's the mayor, is always pretty friendly. I know some people might think it's weird to have a mayor putting shoes on people one day, and being at a parade the next. The way I figure it, the selling of shoes is his secret identity.

It was Saturday morning, so his store had a couple of customers in it, and he was fitting shoes on them. He said "hello" when I walked in. I sat down on a chair and played around with one of those foot measuring things.

At one point he asked if he could help me, but I said I had to talk to him, meaning when other people weren't there. I had to wait, but it was only about twenty minutes.

When the last person went out of the store he sat down beside me. "What's on your mind, Chris?" As I said, in my town everybody knows everybody else.

"Mr. Mayor," I said, "I need to ask you something."

"What about?"

"It's about that Halloween parade last week."

He sort of laughed. "That was the best we've had in a long time. Were you there?"

"No, I couldn't make it," I said. "I saw a picture of you in the paper though, and you were there."

"Right."

"You were giving the prize for the best costume."

"That really was a good one." He shook his head.

"I bet that kid spent a long time on it. I thought it was the best myself. He looked real."

"That's the whole thing," I put in. "Do you know who was wearing the costume?"

The Mayor looked thoughtful for a moment. "That's right. He didn't tell me who he was."

"Could you tell?"

"Nope. Not a bit. I asked but he wouldn't say."

"Did he say anything?"

"Now that you mention it, he didn't. He just shook his head."

I took my time before I asked him the next question. "Then how do you know it was a *boy?*"

He looked at me for a moment with a kind of puzzled look on his face. Then he grinned big, threw back his head, and laughed, really loud. "I guess I don't know," he said in all that laughter.

"So you don't know if it was a boy or a girl?"

"I have to admit I don't." He was still chuckling.

"Could you tell anything about . . . it?"

He was beginning to get interested, and thinking hard. "Nope. Not very much."

"How tall?"

He turned to me. "Stand up next to me and maybe I can remember." I did what he told me. "Wasn't very much bigger than you are."

"Anything else?" I quizzed him.

"Small feet," he said with assurance. "I remember that. About a size three."

"What size do I wear?" I wanted to know.

He gave a quick look at my sneakers. He could tell right away, because he said, "Size four."

There were no further questions in my mind, so I started to leave with a "Thanks a lot."

"How come you're so interested?"

"I just am."

"You've got me curious too. Let me know what you find out. Specially if it's a girl." His own mistake made him laugh again.

I gave him my promise, then went out into the street where I sat down on a bench and tried to figure out if I had learned anything that would help. I decided it was too soon to be sure. Still, with my new facts in mind, I took out my piece of paper that I had been working on the night before, and added some new facts.

12. Muffin's bike changed magically.
13. The warlock did take the bike (I saw it).
14. The warlock has something long, like a braid.
15. The warlock could be a boy or a girl.
16. Whoever it is has to be only a little bigger than me, but with somewhat smaller feet.

I looked over my entire list. I still didn't see how it all fit together, but I was beginning to get some ideas. I didn't like them too much.

Stuffing the list into my back pocket, I started to go home. On the way I made only one stop, George's Toy Store, which is the best place in town for comics. I had my twenty-five cents allowance with me, so I checked up to see if anything interesting had come in. Mr. George is pretty good about kids looking over the comic rack as long as you don't stand there and read the whole thing. But when I saw a new Green Lantern and Flash team-up called, "The Wizard Wins!" I bought it fast and went home.

Coming round the corner to my house I saw a big orange VW bus parked right in front of the house—Eddie's folks' car.

❧ When I saw the car, all my weird suspicions about Eddie came back, and at the same time, my guilty feelings too. I almost didn't want to go inside. I was pretty sure one of his parents would be there, and I was ready to bet that it was about what happened the day before.

I figured I'd just use the patio door out back and go right upstairs. I did go in the back door, but then I had to go through the dining room. There was Eddie's father, my father, and Eddie, sitting around the table.

"Hi, Chris," said John, who was Eddie's father. It was meant to be friendly, but it didn't really come out that way.

"Hello," I said, and kept moving toward the stairs.

"Chris," called my father. "Could you stay here for a moment."

I didn't say anything, just turned around and came up to him, trying like anything to keep from looking at Eddie. I stole enough of a look to see that he wasn't looking at me.

"What's the matter?" I said, up close to my father.

"What happened with you and Eddie yesterday afternoon?" He put his arm around me to show that it wasn't going to be a scolding.

I didn't say anything.

"Did you and Muffin go up to his house?"

"Yeah," I mumbled, not wanting to give anything away.

"Did you have a fight with him?"

"Wasn't a fight."

John leaned across the table. I could tell he was bothered by what had happened. I wondered just how much he knew. "Eddie says that you and Muffin came to our house and accused him of lying about being in the parade because he wasn't on the parade list."

"Is that what happened?" my father cut in.

"Well, sort of," I admitted, relieved that they didn't know the rest.

"I *was* at the parade!" Eddie blurted out.

"You weren't on the list," I returned, just as hot.

John looked down at Eddie. "Do you want to tell him what happened?"

Eddie shook his head hard. I was sure he was going to cry that time.

"Should *I* tell him?" asked John.

Eddie didn't say one thing or another. He was going to let his father decide, though I could tell he wanted John to explain.

"Okay," said John. "I'll say what happened." He turned back to me. "Eddie did go to the parade, but on the way there his tights split and he didn't want to march with his underpants showing."

Eddie turned bright red.

I looked up at my father, and could see that he was trying very hard to hold back a smile. I looked at John. It was the same thing.

"Sure," I countered. "But how do I *know* he was there?"

"Because Rosemary took some pictures of him," said John, taking an envelope out of his pocket. "Do you want to see them?"

It was my turn not to answer. John opened the envelope and pushed a few photos across the table at me. I didn't pick them up, just looked at them where they were. They were of Eddie all right, and you could even see where his tights were torn.

Then something caught my eye. I grabbed up one of the pictures. There was Eddie, right up front. Behind him was a bunch of others in costume. One of them was the warlock.

"That convince you?" my father asked me.

I was staring at the picture.

"Does it?" he repeated.

"It does," I said, but I couldn't take my eyes from the picture.

"Don't you think you should apologize to Eddie?" my father asked me. He was kind of pressing my knee too, just to remind me that the answer was "yes."

I looked up at Eddie and saw that he was looking at me. "I'm sorry," I said, and I meant it too.

"Good," said John, getting up. Then Eddie started to follow him toward the door. I made another decision.

"Can Eddie stay?" I asked.

John looked down at Eddie. "Want to?"

Eddie nodded.

With that John went out with my father, leaving Eddie and me. I took a quick look at his feet. They seemed pretty big to me. We looked at each other. "I really need your help," I said.

In a minute it was all like before, best friends. We ran up the steps to my room.

❧ As soon as we got to my room I shut the door and made Eddie sit down. Then I sat down, but the next thing I did was get up. I wasn't sure how to begin.

"What's it all about?" he finally said to me, when I still hadn't said anything.

"It's so complicated," I tried to explain. "I don't

even know how to tell you. Can you listen for a while?"

"Sure."

Trying to keep everything straight, I reached into my pocket and drew out my long list of facts. I read most of the sixteen points to him, explaining each one. Sometimes he asked me a question, but most of the time he just listened.

When I got to the part about Muffin's parents and what happened to them, I wasn't sure I should even tell him. But that, after all, was perhaps the most important part.

"Can you really keep a secret?" I said to him first.

"Course I can," he insisted.

"Because this is all pretty wild."

"Just tell me," he cut in, impatiently.

Then I let him know what my mother had told me about Muffin. When I was finished I told him that I was sure it *was* all magic, just as Muffin thought.

"I never heard anything like that before," Eddie said.

"Well, then listen to this," I warned him having saved the worst for the last. "I saw the bike last night."

"Where?"

I backed off. "You're not going to believe it."

That got him almost mad. "I will too!"

"Promise?"

"I promise," he pleaded.

Whispering, I told him about my seeing the bike flying across the sky with the warlock pumping away on it like crazy. The only bit I left out was about the thing that looked like a braid. I wasn't ready to tell him that yet.

When I finished I could tell that he was impressed by what I'd told him, and that he believed me, just as he said he would.

"Good thing there was a full moon," he said, "or you never would have seen it."

"I told my father about it."

"What did he say?" Eddie asked, anxiously.

"Said I only dreamed it."

Eddie seemed to like that idea. "Maybe he's right," he said in what I thought was a hopeful way.

"You promised!"

"It's all so crazy," he said.

I reminded him that I hadn't finished.

"Go on."

I told him about my talk with the Mayor and what he had said, that it could have been a boy, or a girl.

"A girl?" said Eddie. "How could that be?" He didn't think girls could do much of anything. "A warlock is a man witch."

"Perfect disguise," I answered him. "The Mayor also said it had small feet."

"Compared to you," he said, "lots of kids have small feet. It could be anyone."

"I don't think it is anyone."

"Who do you think it is?"

I still didn't want to say what was on my mind. I had learned my lesson about accusing people too fast. I only said, "We need more evidence."

"Where are you going to find it?"

"I'm going to go around and ask people about the warlock," I announced. "Maybe they saw something."

Eddie agreed that I had a good idea. We started out right away, going to all my neighbors.

At the first house, right next door, I spoke to Mrs. White, asking her if a warlock had come to her house on Halloween. When she didn't know what I was talking about, I described what the warlock looked like.

"No one came here looking like that," she told me.

We went on to all the other houses. The answer

was always the same. By the time we were done, Eddie was able to sum it up: "That warlock only went to your house."

"And the parade," I added.

We considered this new fact for a long time. "Wait a minute!" Eddie cried. "On that list of yours someone else saw your bike and the warlock!"

I knew at once. "Mr. Podler!"

"I think we should go and speak to him," suggested Eddie.

That left both of us sort of speechless. Mr. Podler was a real crazy character. Most kids tried to keep away from him. He was always making complaints about kids to the police, getting a lot of people in trouble. He also drank a lot, really stank of the stuff. Sometimes you'd see him so drunk he couldn't see right. I knew that my parents had told me to keep out of his way, not even to go near him after he had once complained about me. All the kids had been told pretty much the same thing.

Of course, there were some kids who got so angry with the way he acted that they teased him, which only made matters worse. But it was his own fault.

"You going to go to his house?" Eddie asked me.

"If you come with me," I answered.

Eddie had to think that one over. "I'm not supposed to mess around with him."

"Me neither," I said. "But we've *got* to talk to him. Maybe he can give us some kind of clue."

"We'll only get into trouble," Eddie warned.

"The way I look at it," I said, "is that there's an awful lot of trouble right now. We've got to do something about it. And finding out facts is the way to do it. Anyway, it was your idea," I reminded him.

He was still unsure.

"I'll do the talking," I coached.

"Okay," he finally agreed. We started out right away.

In my town, there is an uptown and a downtown. At least that's the way people talk about it. The uptown side is much nicer with old stone houses and lots of trees. Part of it even gets to be real country-like. That's the end where Eddie lives.

The downtown side is just the opposite. A very long time ago, before I was born, there used to be some kind of factories down there so it doesn't look that nice. The houses aren't so good. A lot look busted, especially near where Mr. Podler lives. In fact, he lives at the most downtown part of all.

To get there you have to go down the main road. Then there's a dirt and gravel side road which goes up a steep hill. Only a few old houses are up there. His house is up that road, the very last one. That was where we were going.

✌ When we got to the

foot of South Pearce Street—where Mr. Podler lives—it was almost eleven thirty, and the sun was pretty bright. The sky was blue as picture-book water, which made us feel better about what we were doing. I'm not sure I would have gone if it had been dark or gloomy.

The street was too steep a hill to bike up, so we just pushed my bike to the top, going past the other two houses there till we got to Mr. Podler's place.

I think I told you what Mr. Bullen's junk yard is like. Well, Mr. Podler's is also a junk yard, but worse, because he lives right in the middle of it. At least Mr. Bullen has a lot of interesting things. Mr. Podler's stuff is not only old, but crummy, no good for anything I can think of. For instance, right up on his porch is a mangle of chicken wire wrapped around an old mattress with its fluffy stuff coming out. That's the kind of junk he has. It sort of makes me sick. I don't know why.

He has chickens around. There must be a law or something about having chickens in town, because nobody else has them except him. I can see why there would be a law because his chickens are dirty and stupid looking. And they're all over the place, about twenty of them. It's as if they were the ones who lived there, not Mr. Podler.

We stood there looking at his house. Most houses in that part of town are wood. His is brick. But most of the bricks are sort of a salmon color, and flaky, like they're sick. Here and there he had slapped on gray cement patches, but that only made things look worse. Plastic sheets, held on by tape, covered the windows. The whole place was ugly.

"You sure you want to do this?" Eddie asked me, as we stood looking at it.

"No, I don't *want* to," I answered in a low voice. "I just think we *have* to."

"Remember," he said, "you do the talking."

"I will. But you stay with me."

I think we must have stood there for five minutes more before we got the nerve to do anything. Finally, it was Eddie who went forward. "Let's get it done with." Eddie's a brave guy.

We went up the old wooden steps and onto the porch where we had to go around the chicken wire mess to get to the door.

I knocked, softly.

"Louder," whispered Eddie.

I did. There was no answer. I gave it another rap, louder this time. I was beginning to feel better just at the thought that he might not even be there.

Still there was no answer.

"Maybe he's dead," Eddie suddenly said.

That kind of talk really scared me. "Don't be stupid," I said quickly, giving the door a final bang. Hanging around for a long time was not what I had in mind.

"Let's go," I said, turning back to the steps.

"Someone's coming," said Eddie. Sure enough, we could hear shuffling on the other side of the door. In a moment the door opened, and Mr. Podler looked out at us.

I don't know how old Mr. Podler is. He looks very old. He's a skinny guy, and his pants were held up by suspenders. That's a good thing, cause they sure would have fallen off otherwise. He wasn't wearing a shirt, but some long-sleeved underwear which didn't look very clean.

Even though his white hair was cut short it looked

messy. And I don't know how you get messy eyebrows, but his were. I suppose if he grew a beard it would be white too, because his face was all prickly white in places he didn't shave.

We must have woken him up, because he was red and bleary-eyed. He didn't look very friendly, that's for sure.

"What the hell do you want?" he demanded when he saw us.

Neither of us said anything. We were both too scared.

"Damn it! What do you want?" he shouted.

Somehow, I found a way to talk. "Mr. Podler, we wanted to ask you something."

"You woke me up."

"We're sorry."

"What time is it?" he asked.

"Almost twelve o'clock."

He looked up toward the sky and rubbed his neck. "I have to eat something," he mumbled, turning his back on us. Then he went into the house, leaving the door open.

Eddie and I looked at each other. Going in there was the last thing we wanted. But when we heard him call out, "Are you coming or not?" we felt we had no choice.

If the outside of his place was a mess, it was nothing compared to what it was like inside. The next time my father says my room is the worst mess he's ever seen, I'll know just where to tell him to look. Stuff was everywhere, piled up, broken, and filthy. As we passed one room, I saw a television set with its glass cracked sitting sideways on an old stuffed chair. There were books too, busted, bent open. Bunches of newspapers were stacked in funny places. Even the walls were falling apart, with big strips of wallpaper peeling right off.

Mr. Podler was standing at the end of the hallway. "You coming?" he called again.

It was kind of dark in there, but we found our way, though not before I tripped over a chair. We went into a kind of kitchen. It must have been a kitchen, because there was food on a table—chicken bones, egg shells, open cans.

Mr. Podler was sitting down next to the table. He had a bottle of something, wine I think, and he was filling a glass.

We watched as he drank, then saw him wipe his hand across his mouth instead of using a napkin. The drink seemed to make him feel better. After a while he didn't drink, just took out some cigarettes and started to smoke.

"What was it you boys wanted?" he said. "Hope you didn't just come here to bother me. Kids are always coming around here to bother me. I have enough on my mind."

He didn't let me speak.

"This place is pretty messy," he said. "I've been having some stomach problems lately, bad ones, which makes it hard for me to keep things in shape. I was going to get to that today."

A chicken wandered into the room as he spoke, then went out. I hesitated, not sure if it was my turn to speak. Before I could, the noon whistle blew in town which made him jump.

"Sorry," he said. "What were you going to say."

"Well, sir, it's about a bike I lost."

"And you think it's up here?" he asked, like it was an accusation.

"No, sir."

"I tell you," he said, already smoking his second cigarette. "I get blamed for more things. But I don't do anything. Just try to mind my own business. I'm getting pretty old you know. I had some kids of my own." He shook his head. "Don't even know where they are. Can you imagine that? I don't even know." Every once in a while he seemed to forget that we were standing there.

"That bike of mine," I started to say again, "was stolen, and the Police Chief told me that you saw it."

"He did?" Mr. Podler's voice sounded surprised, worried.

"That was Halloween," I reminded him.

He rubbed his eyes with his hands. I could see he was still trying to wake up.

"I have to get out of here on Halloween," he informed us. "Kids coming up and bothering me. Parents don't bring up their kids right. They should get a whipping. That's what I did with mine, and they turned out all right. I learned 'em good from wrong."

"Did you see the bike?" I said.

"Like I said, I have to get away from here, so I wasn't even going to be here. I was going to sleep in the woods somewhere out on Fleecy Dale Road. Got a special spot there. Go there sometimes. That's how much people bother me. No privacy." He took another drink.

"The Chief said you saw someone on a bike, that he was in costume, and he flew right over your head."

"Is that what he said?"

"Yes, sir."

"Hard to remember. When you get to my age

things get sort of mixed up. I was in the army once. I'm sorry I can't give you anything to eat. Want some eggs?"

"No, thank you," Eddie said quickly.

"Could you tell us what you saw, Mr. Podler?" I tried again. "We're trying to find my bike."

"Let me see now . . . I'll try. I was going along Fleecy Dale Road that night. Up by the woods, you see. That's right. Now I remember. And somewhere —by that bridge, you know—I was just walking along, and when I looked up, by golly, I saw a bike coming right at me."

"Was it green?" I asked.

My question calmed him down. "I don't know. I can't remember all those things. It was dark. And you know," he said in a whisper, "maybe I'd drunk a little bit too much. I do that sometimes. Keeps you warm, understand. That's the reason for it."

"Did you see anyone with the bike?" I asked, hardly able to keep from yelling at him.

Mr. Podler took another drink before he answered. "You might say so. Yes."

"Who?"

"Mind you, it was hard to see. Pretty dark. All those trees standing around. I seen that bike coming right at me. Sure, there must have been someone.

You can't have a bike come at you without a person on it, can you?" he asked.

"What did he look like?" demanded Eddie.

"Damned if I remember," said Mr. Podler, shaking his head. "All checkered or something."

"The warlock!" I cried.

"The what?"

"Is that all you saw?" I wanted to know.

"I saw it coming right at me. I took a swing. Off it flew. I heard a crash . . ."

"A crash?"

"Something like that. Kids pulling their tricks on me, that's what it was," he said suddenly in an angry voice, as if it were happening again. "It got me so mad I went right back and told the police. Kids are always bothering me. You boys seem nice, though."

There didn't seem to be much point in staying any longer. He would have talked on, but we kept saying "thank you" as we backed up and went outside. We didn't say a word to each other till we got to the bottom of the hill.

"What do you think?" I asked Eddie.

"Sure sounded like the warlock."

"It sure did."

"But it made me think of something else," he added.

"That coat Muffin wears," he said, "isn't that sort of checkered?"

I knew he was going to say that.

&ko; Eddie and I went back

to my house slowly. I wasn't sure what he was thinking, but I could guess pretty well. I knew what was going through my head and it made me nervous. Though why Muffin should want my bike I couldn't imagine, no more than I could understand why she should want to steal her costume, *if* that happened.

The only thing that made any sense to me was that maybe the bike *was* a magical bike. I had always thought its green color was special. I used it as if it were. Now maybe it would turn out that it really was magical. Not that I was absolutely sure what a magical bike would do for her, or anyone. What connection it had with her parents was not clear to me.

Now, while I was trying to work all that out, I was also thinking other things. I mean, just the day before I had thought it was Eddie who had taken the bike. It really seemed as if he had. Aside from being shown that I was wrong, I knew I had made him feel real bad. That was wrong. And it was my fault. If you think someone is wrong, or did a bad thing, you have to ask them right out, or it's not fair. Somewhere along the line I was going to have to ask Muffin directly, and there were still too many other things I needed to know before I did that. It may be better to ask someone right out if they are a . . . witch, or something, but you better have a lot of right answers first.

When we got to my house I asked Eddie if he wanted to have lunch with me. Instead of answering, he said, "Do you think it was Muffin all the time?"

I tried to duck the question. "Maybe."

"Then it figures she would try to blame me," he put in, bitterly.

I hadn't even thought of that. It sort of was she who gave me the idea that Eddie was guilty.

"Sure," he went on. "If she was the one, she'd want you to think it was someone else, your best friend, for one thing."

"I suppose so."

"And I bet that's just why she did it, just to get me in trouble with you."

I had to listen to what Eddie was saying, but I kept reminding myself that he didn't like her very much to begin with, which wasn't fair. Of course, I had the idea she didn't like him either.

"What are you going to do about it?" he demanded, waiting for an answer.

"I don't know," I admitted.

"Seems to me," he said, "that you should do something. She was only making trouble for us."

"Maybe she wasn't," I tried to say. "Maybe it has something to do with her parents, and all that other stuff." But as I said that I knew I was only trying to find a way out.

Eddie looked at me hard. "You know, you can't have two best friends who don't like each other. That's all I can say." And it was all, for he just turned around and started to walk home. "Let me know what you're going to do," he called back, leaving me standing there.

I have to admit I felt he was right, yet, at the same time, I felt he was wrong. Those are hard kinds of feelings to get together. It was just as well that he left me alone.

When I went into the house my mother and father were there, just finishing their lunch. I looked over what they had been eating, and it seemed all right, except there was no peanut butter on the table.

I got a plate and the peanut butter, and sat down.

"Where've you been?" my father asked, as if nothing was going on.

"With Eddie."

"You friends again?" he wanted to know.

"Sure." I didn't really want to talk to him about the business, but he was in one of his teaching moods.

"You have to be careful when you accuse people, you know. You have to get . . ."

". . . the right questions before you get the wrong answers," I finished for him, in the best sarcastic voice I could manage. That annoyed him, because he stopped talking, which was fine with me.

I had decided to talk it out with Mike, so I tried to eat as fast as I could just to get away. But my mother said I'd kill myself if I didn't slow down.

"You going to see Muffin today?" she asked me right out of nowhere. That made me swallow my food the wrong way.

"I don't want to talk about it."

She lifted up one eyebrow which was a trick she had. "Oh, I thought you were good friends."

I slammed my fork down on the table. "I don't want to talk about it," I yelled. That really made them sit up.

96

"You can say so politely," my mother said in her special calm voice which she uses only when she's furious.

"I'm sorry," I apologized, going back to my food.

Things were silent for a while. "I found out about that coat of hers," my mother put in.

I did want to know about that, but now I couldn't say so. So I said nothing.

"Would you like to know?" she asked.

"If you want to tell me," I said, trying not to be too eager.

"It's probably machine woven after all," my mother explained. "But the design is Druid. It's very unusual."

I couldn't have cared less, but I figured it was one way out of the subject of Muffin. "What is Druid?" I asked.

"The Druids are a mysterious people from England," said my mother. "Some people think of them as ancient magicians. I gather some people still believe in Druidism."

"That's right," put in my father. "Some of the ideas we associate with witchcraft come from the Druids. Witches, and that sort of thing . . ."

I wasn't listening any more. I had jumped off my chair and was out of the door, heading for Muffin's house. I don't even remember getting on my bike.

All I remember is that I went fast, real fast. I covered the few blocks to where she lives as fast as I had ever traveled.

There was so much going through my head that I couldn't get any of it straight. All I knew was that now I had all the answers *I* needed. *She* was the one, and I was going to tell her I knew it. More than that I was mad, mad for being tricked and fooled. And I wanted my bike back, no matter what she could do to me.

I pedaled so fast that when I came up to her house I forgot to think of how I was going to accuse her. What made that bad was that there she was, sitting on the steps in front of her house, just as quietly as anything.

"Hi, Chris," she called to me. "I was hoping you'd come. I've figured out who the warlock is."

❧ When I drove up, furious, sure I knew exactly what had happened, and Muffin said, "I've figured out who the warlock is," I just stood there, not knowing what to say. I must have looked pretty freaked out, because she laughed.

Finally, I got my mouth to say, "Who?"

"It's not Eddie," she started off.

That gave me some time to think. So I said, "How did you come to that?"

"I remembered something you had told me, that Eddie came to your house on Halloween night in a Batman costume."

"That's right, he did."

"You also said the warlock came to your house."

She was right. That's the way it had happened.

"Okay," she went on. "Can you remember how much time there was between the two of them coming?"

"Couldn't have been too long."

"How long? Exactly."

I thought as hard as I could. "Five minutes, maybe."

"Well," she said, "then it couldn't have been him. He couldn't have gotten out of the one costume and come back so soon in the other. Where was he going to change? He lives two miles from your house, right? I don't think he would change in the street, do you?"

"No, I don't," I said, sore at myself for not thinking of all that in the first place. "But I knew it wasn't him anyway," I let her know.

"How did you work it out?" she asked, not seeming the least bit troubled.

"Remember how he said his mother took pictures of him?"

"Yes."

"Well, she did," I told her. "I saw them. He wasn't in the parade, but he watched it. He ripped his tights, that's why."

"There you are then. I was right," she said matter-of-factly.

"But you said you knew who it was," I suddenly remembered.

"I think so."

"Who?" I demanded.

"Just as simple as anything she said, "Mr. Bullen."

"Mr. Bullen!" I cried. The idea just completely knocked me all sorts of ways inside my head. "How do you get that?"

She didn't answer me right away, but wrapped her Druid coat around her a little tighter. It made her pale face, surrounded by black hair, seem so small, almost as if she were a fairy.

"I don't have much proof, yet," she admitted. "We'll have to get some more. But, didn't you tell me you got your bike, your green bike, from him in the first place?"

"That's right, I did."

"You told me that he didn't really want you to take it." ·

I remembered that.

"Was he surprised when you told him it was stolen?"

"It's hard to say with him," I said. "He's got such an old-looking face, I never really know what he's thinking."

"How old?"

"Ages. I don't know."

"When you went back," she continued, "didn't he almost *give* you a new one? You paid just about as much as mine, and mine isn't nearly so good. Look at it. It has all those rust spots."

I turned to look. Now that it was out of the sun again, I could see the rust spots. She was right.

"I think," she went on, "he was just feeling sorry for what he'd done, and was sort of giving you a new bike, just to make you feel better and to like him."

"What about the costume?"

"How big is he?" she asked me in return, but she acted as if she knew the answer.

"Not so big. Only a little bigger than I am," I was forced to admit. "But why would he even bother with the costume?"

"That's the best part," she said, smiling. "Think about it. He can't very well go through the streets and just take a bike, your bike. What would be the best way in the whole world to hide himself?"

"A costume!"

"So you see," she finished, "that's why."

"Cause if he came to my door and wasn't in costume," I pointed out, "we would have recognized him."

"That's why he didn't give his name in the parade," said Muffin. "Any kid would have been glad to let everybody know he won, but a grownup wouldn't have been allowed to."

"He's got small feet!" I shouted.

"I suppose he does," said Muffin. "Does that mean anything?"

I quickly told her about my visit with the Mayor, and she agreed it helped to prove that Mr. Bullen was the one.

"Remember," she said, "how he wanted my coat?"

Now that she mentioned it, I did. With that however, it came to be my turn to ask the questions. I wasn't sure I should tell her the things I had learned about her. It didn't seem the time. But when she mentioned the coat, I couldn't help but ask her why she thought Mr. Bullen wanted it.

She didn't answer right away, but huddled down inside of her coat without even looking at me. I just let her make up her own mind.

"If I tell you, will you promise not to tell?"

"Promise."

"You'd better sit down," she said, and her face looked very serious. Then she told me the whole story about her parents, how her mother was just gone one day, and how bad her father felt. "He kept saying that the magic had gone. When I asked him about that, he didn't explain much. He just kept saying that if he could find a way to get back the magic, she would come home. And she would have, cause as bad as he felt, my mother must have felt worse, since she was away, and at least he was home."

"What kind of magic was it?" I asked Muffin.

"He wouldn't say, only that it was his fault they had lost it. That if he hadn't been thinking so much just about himself all the time, he would have noticed it was going. He was very angry at himself for losing it."

"It must have been powerful magic to make her go," I agreed.

"Then, one day, he told me he had to go and find the magic and make it work again. He said he could find it, that it wouldn't take long. He asked me if I would mind staying with my aunt—that's his sister —till he did find it."

"Did you mind?"

"I did," she said, "but he said it would only be for a couple of weeks, and I wanted the magic to be found so we could be all together again. I told him I'd look out for the magic too."

"What did he say to that?"

"He kind of smiled and said I was already full of magic."

"He really said that?"

She nodded.

"What about the coat?"

She scrunched up real small when I asked her that, and when she spoke her voice was smaller. "I stole it," she said.

"Stole it!"

"Just before my father took me to the bus I went into my mother's closet. I was sort of cold anyway, and when I saw it there I took it. So I put it on. And I kept it."

"It is magic," I whispered.

"How do you know?"

I told her all about the Druids, just as my folks had explained it to me.

She didn't change her expression. "I didn't know that. But I'm not surprised. It keeps me warm. And sometimes, when I'm feeling kind of lonely, it makes me feel like my parents are hugging me. That's why I don't mind that it's a little big."

It all made sense to me.

"But don't tell anybody about this at all," she said.

"I won't," I promised, and neither of us said much for a while. Then it came back to me about Mr. Bullen. "What do you think Mr. Bullen has to do with it all?"

"The way I figure it," said Muffin, thinking as she talked, "since he's the warlock, maybe he's the one who stole the magic from my folks. Somehow, I don't know how, your bike is the magical thing we need. He needs to have it to keep them away. We need to get it so they can come back."

Then, in a new voice, really glad it wasn't Muffin, I said, "It must have been him I saw on the bike last night."

"Where?"

"Riding across the sky. He was on my bike."

"That's the best proof so far," she agreed. After a moment she said, "I think we better go up to Mr. Bullen's place. I bet we find something more."

"Do you have to ask your aunt?"

"She went somewhere. She told me to wait for her, but I won't."

We weren't happy about what we were doing. We weren't scared either. We just knew what we had to do, so we got on our bikes and headed for Mr. Bullen's.

✌ As we raced along

up to Mr. Bullen's I kept thinking how stupid I was not to have realized that it was him all along. It made so much sense, from the way he looked, to the way he had acted. He never did want me to have that green bike, but since I chose it, he had to sell it to me. Once he did that, he had to steal it back. No other way. It made all the sense in the world.

"Let's decide how we're going to do this," I called to Muffin, skidding to a stop when we got close.

"Just ask him," she suggested.

"I want to search for some more evidence first," I told her. "Real evidence."

"But he'll have hidden it," Muffin pointed out.

"In that place of his it could be anywhere. I mean, it's absolutely the best hiding place in the whole world."

"Well," I insisted, "we can't just ask him. He's the warlock, remember. If he gets angry, he might even do something to us. He made your parents disappear, didn't he?"

That made Muffin thoughtful. "I guess we better have a plan," she agreed.

"What are we going to be looking for?" I asked.

"Anything. The bike, the costume, the trophy."

"What trophy?"

"That prize he got for the best costume."

"Right," I remembered. "Even if that was the only thing we found we'd have enough evidence."

"He might even still want the costume, but not the trophy cup," Muffin pointed out.

"Still, that's just the kind of thing that would be easy to hide up there," I said.

"What if he asks us what we're doing?" Muffin wondered.

I had an idea. "I'll tell him I'm looking for radio parts for my brother."

We covered the rest of the distance quickly, but when we got there, Mr. Bullen was standing right at the entranceway with some other people, talking to them. He gave us a funny look as we approached.

"Try not to look like you think he's the warlock," Muffin warned me. I tried, but I was still afraid that he would know why we were there the minute he saw us.

We pushed open the gate and started to walk toward the mounds of things. Suddenly, Mr. Bullen called out to us.

"Hya! What you doing up here?"

We stopped. "Looking for radio things for my brother," I called back.

"That's over there," he let me know, pointing in the opposite direction from the way we were going.

We felt we had to go where he told us, along rows of more kinds of stuff than I could believe. It was so confused it made me wonder if Mr. Bullen himself knew all the things he had.

"Great hiding places," Muffin whispered to me.

"Gives me the creeps," was my answer. I kept feeling that we were being watched, even though I could hear Mr. Bullen's voice some distance away, trying to sell the people an old table. We kept going. I could see the old radios just ahead.

We started looking, and we must have been at it fifteen minutes, just going through the junk, when Muffin cried, "Look!" She pointed to a freaky twist of bed springs lying on its side, folded around like a tube, its open end toward us. In the middle of the tube was a bundle of cloth which had been wrapped around something—something shiny, flashing in the sun.

I got down on my hands and knees and put my arm far into the tube hole, trying to grab the cloth away from the shiny thing. And I did, a little. Enough to see what it was. It was a trophy cup, bright yellow in color, like gold.

Muffin squatted down beside me. "Is that it?" she whispered.

"I think so," I said, not daring to raise my voice either. I tried to reach in deeper, but couldn't. The cup just hung in all that metal web.

"What's that around it?" I asked her.

She shook her head, then looked around till she found a long window-shade rod which she poked through the springs at the cup. That managed to bring the cup an inch or two closer, only still not near enough to grab. But when she had moved things around she had turned over the cloth wrapping. You could see its other side now. It had a checkered pattern.

"The costume!" she cried.

"How did it get in there?"

Muffin stood up and looked over the springs. "He must have thrown it in," she decided.

I tried to pull the bed springs apart so Muffin could get to the trophy. It helped a little, but I wasn't strong enough. Then the two of us tried to pull out the whole pile, but couldn't. Again I tried to reach in, only that time I used my foot.

"Hey! What you doing?" Mr. Bullen appeared from behind a bunch of bathtubs.

We drew back instantly.

Mr. Bullen glared angrily at us, mostly at me. "Kids aren't allowed around here alone. It's dangerous here. You know that. Things are always falling. You're going to get hurt if you don't watch out. Then what would your mother say?" He was really mad.

I hardly dared to look at him.

Muffin did though, and it was the most amazing thing. She said, "we were trying to get something in there."

Mr. Bullen turned to look at her. "What's your name?"

"Muffin."

"Muffin," he repeated, with something like a smile on his face. "That's a funny name. Do you have a last name?"

I sort of gave her a nudge. She didn't need me to tell her. She said nothing.

"Oh yes," he said, his eyes narrowing. "You're the one with the coat." Then quickly, he turned to me. "What was it you wanted?"

"Well," I stammered, "there's a trophy in there. We wanted to look at it."

"A trophy?" he said, acting surprised and bending down to look into the tangled mess. When he did I glanced at his feet. They were small.

"Why do you want that?" he said to me, looking over his shoulder.

"Just do."

He stood up, brushing off his trousers. "Forget it. It's too far in there."

"Couldn't we try," I asked.

Mr. Bullen's eyes got angry again. "What's so important about it? I've got plenty of trophies over on the other side. People bring them to me."

"We want that one," said Muffin, boldly.

Mr. Bullen shook his head. "Come on. I'll show you the others." He started to go. We refused to move.

"Now, look here," he yelled at us. "I can't have kids around. It's not allowed. You're going to get hurt," he warned. "Go on. Get out!"

But as he said that, a car pulled up to the yard, and a man got out. Mr. Bullen seemed torn as to which way to go. As he watched the man go farther into the lot, he gave us a final, angry word of advice. "I'm warning you for the last time. It's dangerous." With that he went after the man.

We still didn't move.

"That *must* be it!" said Muffin urgently. "We've got to get it."

I looked around desperately trying to figure out a way to reach it.

"Can you hold up the spring?" she asked me. "Then I can crawl under."

"You'll get caught in there," I told her.

"Come on! We don't have a lot of time."

The two of us grabbed the end of the bed springs and lifted. With the two of us lifting we hoisted it all up about two feet off the ground. Inside, the cup dropped to the ground with a "plink."

"Now, hold it!" she called. "I'm going to crawl under." I braced myself as she let go. The weight of the metal came down hard, and for a moment I was sure it was going to rip out of my hands. But somehow I set myself, and held on, even though it hurt.

Muffin, hardly waiting to see if I could hold it, dropped down on her hands and knees, then on her belly, and slithered, snake-like, right underneath.

"Hurry!" I screamed. "It's slipping."

"Got it!" she called, but when she yanked the costume free I almost lost my grip.

"Faster!"

She squirmed out. Not any too soon, either, for the weight of the springs had gotten to be too much. The whole thing smashed down.

Muffin, dirty from head to foot, held up the trophy and costume bundle triumphantly. "Got them!" she cried with a big smile. It occurred to me right then that I had never seen her smile before. It was nice.

"Now we have to get it out of here," I said, but she had already slipped the stuff under her coat.

I stopped short. "We can't do this. It's stealing!"

"He stole, didn't he?" she countered.

We heard Mr. Bullen's voice. "Hey! You kids still here?"

I didn't argue any more. We ran the other way, out of the yard, completely avoiding Mr. Bullen as he came running after us. We jumped on our bikes.

"Hey! Where you going?"

But we were already gone, pumping like crazy to get away from him.

I led the way back into town and across a couple of streets until I pulled up behind the Main Street Bank. Muffin, close behind, came up next to me.

"Got it?" I asked her, breathless.

She didn't say a word. She just pulled open her coat and plucked out the trophy and costume. The cup was slightly dented and didn't fit too well on its plastic stand, but on the cup was written BEST COSTUME and a date, that very year.

"That *is* it, isn't it?" said Muffin, and her voice sounded a little scared. It was weird to think that it really was the one we were looking for.

Then I laid out the warlock costume with its checkered cape.

"That's mine," she said.

"Now," I said, "if we could only get my bike back, I bet we'd have the magic too."

"It's probably hidden up there," she said, "all crashed to bits and dumped somewhere."

The minute she said that I had the answer.

"Oh no," I said. "I know exactly where it is!"

ᴖ When I told Muffin

I knew where the bike was, she just looked at me as if I was crazy.

"I only figured it out," I quickly told her, "when you said crash and dump."

"What do you mean?"

"It was something Mr. Podler told me this morning."

"Who's he?"

I told her as much as I knew about Mr. Podler. Who he was, where he lived, and most of all about how he had seen the bike. I repeated what he had said, in particular about something checkered and the flying bike crashing.

"You know," I said, "when he said 'checkered' it made me think it was you he was talking about, what with your coat looking checkered and all."

"Did you really think so?" she asked. For a moment I had the feeling she was even pleased that I thought she was a magical person.

"Only a little bit," I lied.

She smiled. "Is that why you came over before?"

"Sort of."

"I wish it were me," she said laughing. "If I had all that magic that Mr. Bullen has I'd . . ." She didn't finish.

"What would you do?"

"I'd get my mother and father back, for one."

"Then what?"

"I'd have fun, I guess." Her smile faded away. "But I'm not, and anyway, we've got to get the bike. Where is it?"

"Well," I began, "he said he had been up Fleecy Dale Road near . . ." She never let me finish.

"That swimming place!" she cried out. "I knew there was something special about it."

"It's so green," I agreed. "That crash and flying that he saw was the warlock flying the bike right into the pond with a splash."

"I bet there's an underground passage there," she added.

"Right. So that must be the spot where the bike is," I concluded. "We're going to have to fish it out."

That ended the discussion about where the bike was. Next came the problem of how to get the bike out from its underwater hiding place.

We must have thought of a hundred different ways, none of which we could do—like Scuba diving—when I finally had a good idea. "My grandpa gave me a toy anchor," I told her. "It's only about this big," I explained, holding my hands a foot apart. "But it's metal."

"Can you get it?"

"I think so. It was on my toy shelf. We can stop on the way to the bridge."

"You get it," she said. "I never told my aunt that I was going. She'll get sore if I don't tell her something."

Having agreed to meet by the school, we each went to our own homes. It was only a matter of minutes for me. I raced inside, and upstairs.

"Chris! Is that you?" I heard my mother call.

I paid no attention, but went through my stuff looking for that anchor. It took a while and I wasn't helped by my mother who kept yelling up at me saying she had something important to tell me. I saw the anchor, grabbed it, raced down the steps, and pretended not to see her.

"Chris!" She made a grab at me. "Something wonderful has happened."

She could have told me Wonder Woman was coming, it wouldn't have stopped me.

"Muffin's aunt called and . . ."

"Later. I'm going to Eddie's!" I shouted, and was out of the door and onto my bike before she could say or do anything. I heard her calling after me furiously, but I was gone.

Muffin was waiting in the schoolyard when I arrived.

"Get it?" she asked.

I held up the anchor. "Tell your aunt?"

"I didn't go home. I was afraid she'd say I couldn't go out again."

None of that mattered to us. Nothing could stop us now. We raced down toward Fleecy Dale Road.

As we were going Muffin suddenly realized that we'd forgotten all about a rope. "Do you have one at home?" She called to me.

I shook my head. "I can't go back. Maybe Eddie has one," I suggested. She nodded.

We got to the bridge in about fifteen minutes, put the bikes up on their kick stands, and looked down into the still, deep, green pool.

It was so quiet, there was no sound at all. Nothing on the water moved. Muffin said it looked like a cat's eye in the night.

"It's so green," I said, trying to look down into the bottom.

"Like your bike."

The stillness made us feel a little nervous. Having come so far, it suddenly didn't seem as if it was going to be all that easy.

"There might be things down there," I said.

"Imps, most likely," she agreed. "You have to be careful with them."

"Don't want them to get angry," I agreed. "They probably guard the bike."

"And at night," said Muffin, "Mr. Bullen comes right here. He dives down, brings up the bike, and flies into the sky. Maybe he visits my mom and dad —wherever he put them. Then, when he's finished tormenting them, and making them feel sad, he comes back and dives into the pond. That's when Mr. Podler saw him."

"We'd better get that rope," I said. "Come on with me."

We took our bikes and rode the short distance to Eddie's house. He was outside, kicking around a soccer ball. I called to him, and he ran over, but when he saw Muffin, he stopped. An angry look came over his face.

"It's all right," I yelled up to him. "We've figured it all out."

He refused to come a step closer. "She going to get me in trouble again?" he wanted to know.

"I didn't think it was you," said Muffin on her own.

"You sure acted as if you did."

"I'm sorry," she pleaded. "I really am."

"She means that," I let him know. "And anyway, we found out who really took the costume and the bike."

"Who?"

"Mr. Bullen."

"You're kidding."

"Got proof," I insisted, while Muffin held up the costume for Eddie to see. "And we know exactly where the bike is," I added.

"Where?"

"In the swimming place, under the bridge."

That got him. He was really interested, so I told him how it all worked out. Muffin told him about her parents and why we had to get the bike back.

"All we have to do," I told him, "is get the bike back and then we'll have the magic. We'll break Mr. Bullen's magic and Muffin says we'll be able to get her parents back."

"But we need a rope," Muffin reminded me.

"I'll get one," said Eddie. Turning, he ran right toward his barn, coming back in a moment with his bat-rope which was just about perfect.

The three of us raced back to the bridge where we tied the anchor onto the rope like it was a fish hook. That done, we gradually lowered it into the water.

By then the sun had begun to go down, so there were long shadows coming across the pond, like grabbing fingers. It made everything look dark, angry almost. We could feel a breeze. I shivered.

"How far is it till I hit the water?" I asked, lowering the anchor down. I was surprised to hear myself whispering.

Eddie and Muffin, leaning over the bridge, gave me instructions. "About four more feet."

Slowly, I let the anchor down. When it hit the water the splash made me jump.

Somewhere in the woods a crow began to caw again and again.

"Get it to the deep part," was Eddie's advice. I did what he told me.

With the two of them guiding me, I continued to let the rope out slowly, down along the cliff side of the pond where it was deepest. Sometimes I could feel the anchor bumping against the rock.

Suddenly, it hit bottom. "Can't go down any more," I cried.

"Now walk along the bridge and drag it on the bottom," Muffin urged.

I began to do as she said, and I hadn't gone but five feet when I felt the anchor snag on something. "Got something!"

"Pull it!" they yelled.

Gripping the rope with both hands, I began to haul in the anchor. I called to them for help. It was so heavy I had the feeling that someone was pulling it down from under the water. Both of them began to pull with me. Little by little, whatever it was we had caught onto came closer to the surface.

"Pull!" I pleaded. Eddie kept running to the side of the bridge to see what was happening. After a few more yanks he saw a shadow form right under the water. "Little bit more!" he yelled, and we pulled harder than ever.

With a tremendous heave, it broke the surface of the water. It was a branch. We were about to let it drop when Eddie called out, "Hold it! There's something on it."

Muffin held the rope while I peered over the bridge. I could hardly believe what I saw. It looked like a body.

"Pull!" I cried, and all three of us gave it a huge pull. The branch came completely up out of the water. We peered down at it again.

"That's my jacket!" I shouted, pointing to the thing that looked like a body. I was as excited as if I had been looking for it. Its checkered pattern was all covered with a green slimy mud, but it was my jacket that I had lost somewhere, there was no doubt about that.

We pulled the branch up the rest of the way, grabbed it, and swung it onto the bridge. Then we took off the jacket, hung it up to dry, pulled the anchor off the branch, and flung it down into the water again. Only that time we got it a little under the bridge. When it hit the bottom I began to drag it along the bottom as I had before.

We caught onto something almost immediately, and when we started to pull it seemed even heavier than the branch.

"Another branch, I bet," said Eddie. We pulled anyway, as hard as we could. It came up slowly, only gradually showing any form—stick-like lines which made it look like another branch.

"More!" urged Muffin.

The final pull was always the hardest. All three of us braced ourselves and yanked. Up it came out of the water. "It's a bike!" Muffin yelled.

When Muffin shouted that out, we were so excited I think we almost dropped the whole thing. We didn't though, but managed to get the bike up on the bridge. Then we stood it up on the roadway.

"Careful," I warned them. "If that's mine, it doesn't have a good kick stand. It's always falling down."

The bike was dirty, rusty in some spots, but it *was* a bike and it looked like mine. Carefully, we began to wipe off the mud and green stuff. As we did, it's own color began to show through—green.

"Is it?" Muffin whispered, hardly daring to speak.

"Nobody else's," I assured her.

"Then we've got his magic," she announced. And it was a good thing too, cause even as she said that two cars slowly drove up to the bridge and stopped right next to us. In the first car was the Police Chief. In the second was my mother and my brother Mike. In the back seat of my mother's car was Mr. Bullen.

&⁊ When we saw all of those people we stood behind my green bike, knowing it would protect us if necessary. Nobody said to, but we all did it just the same.

The first one out of the cars was the Police Chief. He didn't seem to be in a great hurry. He started off with a friendly, "Hi, Chris," but I was suspicious all the same. When he nodded to Muffin and Eddie I said "hello" back, but the others didn't.

Then came Mike and my mother. One look at her and I could tell something was up, but I couldn't be sure what. Then came Mr. Bullen, looking real small next to the other grownups. He sort of hung back, not saying anything.

Standing there, Chief Byers looked us over, looked at the bike, the water, and the muck all over the place. Then he shook his head, but what that meant I wasn't sure.

"Greetings," said my mother, speaking first. "What's going on, Chris?" The way she said it I could tell she wasn't fooling around.

We didn't say anything.

"I asked you something, Chris," my mother said.

"Nothing," I answered. "I got my bike back."

"Is that right," said the Chief. "Where abouts was it?"

"Down in the stream here," I told them.

"In the pond?" cried my brother. You could see he was surprised.

"How'd it get there?" the Chief wanted to know.

I didn't know what to say to that. In fact, I wasn't sure we should say anything. It's pretty serious to say that someone is a warlock, specially if that very warlock is standing right there in front of you.

My mother turned to Muffin. "Did you know your aunt is looking all over for you?"

Muffin shook her head.

"Now, look here," the Chief cut in. "Chris, your

mother called me right after Mr. Bullen here came to see her. Seems you kids were in his yard when you weren't supposed to be. Did you take something from down there?"

I felt awful. I knew we shouldn't have taken that stuff. So I just stood there, not saying anything. Fact is, I didn't know what to say.

But Muffin spoke up. "Yes, we went up there. And we did take something."

"Muffin," said my mother. "I'm surprised at you. I'm surprised at you all." But she was looking at me.

"That's stealing, you know," said the Chief. "And stealing is against the law. I'm sure you know that."

Muffin was not going to be fooled with. She stood up tall. "It's not stealing when you take back something that was stolen."

I could see Mr. Bullen standing a little ways back as if he didn't need any explanations.

"Now what does that mean?" my mother wanted to know. "Eddie," she asked, "were you in this too?"

"Sorta," he said, which I thought was pretty gutsy, because he could have gotten out of the whole thing if he had wanted to. But he stuck with us.

"You kids will have to do some more explaining, I'm afraid," said the Chief.

"It's all because of him!" Muffin said suddenly, and she pointed right to Mr. Bullen.

"Now please explain that," said the Chief patiently.

"He used magic to steal my parents," began Muffin.

"And the magic was my bike," I said, finding my tongue now that Muffin had begun to talk. "But then I bought it from him, even though he didn't want me to."

"So he had to steal it back," put in Eddie.

"In order to do that he stole my warlock costume," said Muffin. "He did that to be disguised. He only went to Chris's house and made sure they didn't recognize him."

"That's when he stole the bike back from me," I said.

Eddie continued. "But then he was at the parade, and won the prize for the best costume."

"That's why he didn't dare tell who he was, cause that would have given the whole thing away," I explained. "The Mayor said it was somebody like him, small and all, with little feet."

"Mr. Podler saw him flying the bike right into the stream under the bridge," said Eddie.

"And I saw him flying through the sky with it," I announced.

"He hid the costume and the trophy cup in his junk yard where nobody could find it," said Muffin.

"But we found it, and we took it back, and that's all the proof we need."

"That's how we got the bike back," I explained, "by figuring all that out."

"It's the magic I need to get my mother and father back," Muffin concluded.

There it was. We had said it all, every bit of it. For a moment nobody said anything. The Chief looked at my mother, then at Mr. Bullen. For a second I thought the Chief was going to laugh, but he didn't. "I'm afraid," he said, "you're going too fast for me. You say that Mr. Bullen did all that?"

"He's a warlock," explained Eddie.

With that accusation the Chief looked very serious. "But I don't understand why the bike was down in the stream here," he said.

"There's a whole secret cavern down there," explained Muffin. "It's where he keeps things, like the bike."

"Right," I said. "Mr. Bullen is in charge of it all. He's the head witch."

"Mr. Bullen, did you get all that?" asked the Chief.

We all turned to look at Mr. Bullen. He had the funniest look on his face, as though he were trying to find a way out of the situation. But as I looked at him I just knew we were right. I was no longer frightened of him, though, not since we had the bike.

"I'll tell ya . . ." he began, but he didn't finish. He kept looking at us. Then he did the most surprising thing of all.

He laughed.

It wasn't just a short, simple laugh, it was a long, big one, the kind of laugh that sounds funny. A you-almost-have-to-laugh-yourself kind of laugh. I know I almost did. He laughed so hard he had tears running down his cheeks. And when he finally stopped, he managed to say, "No, I'm no warlock. Never heard of such a thing." Then he began to laugh that laugh again.

Muffin got really mad. "He's lying!"

"We better hold on for one minute," put in the Chief. "This whole thing is too crazy. Where do you live?" he asked Muffin.

"On Delevan Street."

"Well," said the Chief, "I'm not going to stand here talking about witches and warlocks, and blocking the road. We're all going to go to your house and talk to your folks too."

"Her folks aren't there," I said.

"Oh? Where are they?"

"They were taken away by magic," said Muffin.

"That being the case who do you live with?"

"My aunt, Miss Richter. But now that we've got the bike, my folks will be able to come back."

The Chief shook his head. "I don't want to get into that here. We've got to move away from this place. Let's go back to town."

"I think that's an excellent idea," my mother agreed. "I'm sure Muffin's aunt will be very worried by now. Eddie, you go get your father or mother."

"I'd better take Mr. Bullen here," said the Chief. "The kids can go with you."

"Aren't you going to arrest him?" demanded Muffin.

"Don't you worry. When we get back to town we're going to work this all out," the Chief answered her.

After loading the bikes in the back of our car, we started to get in.

"You don't need me," announced Mike. "I'll walk home." I could see he was sort of upset with our proof about the magic.

"You get into the car," snapped my mother. "I want no more chasing around."

My mother drove us back. We were followed first by the Chief, then by Eddie and his mother.

All the way back to town nobody said anything,

though Muffin and I, in the back seat, kept looking at each other. We knew we were right. Mike, in the far back, said nothing.

When we got to Muffin's house, we all got out. Muffin led the way, running up to her porch, but before she reached the door it opened. A man and a woman stood there smiling at her. Muffin stopped when she saw them as if they were ghosts or something. Talk about magic.

Then, with a scream, which was half-happy and half-scared, she ran forward and hugged them, first one, then the other, then both at the same time. I looked to my mother for an explanation, but she only grinned.

In the midst of all the hugging, Muffin broke away and turned to us. "That's final proof," she announced. "These are my parents."

We *had* got them back. The magic of the bike worked.

∾ I guess it must seem crazy. But Muffin was right. Having her parents there was the final proof, even though they seemed a little puzzled by all the people gathered around. In fact, after Muffin had said that, her mother said, "What proof? What is this all about?" She kept looking at the whole mob of us.

"Dad said the magic left your marriage," Muffin explained. "But it's come back now, hasn't it?"

"Did I say that?" her father asked.

Muffin nodded.

Her parents looked at one another. It was her father who knelt down, and took hold of her. "Now look here, Muffin, we're going to have to try and find some other kinds of ways to keep us all together. We're just going to have to depend on a little bit more real love and respect. I'm afraid there is no more magic."

Muffin shook her head. "It did come back, and it came back because I got it back, with Chris, who's my best friend. Eddie too, he's my friend, and he helped. And that man, Mr. Bullen, he's the warlock who stole it."

While she was explaining things, a woman, looking a little bit like Muffin's father, but older, had come out on the porch. I figured her to be the aunt Muffin had been staying with.

"I'm afraid Muffin's always going on about magic," the aunt said, as if it was something wrong about Muffin. "I've tried to get her to stop." She shook her head. I never did like her much.

Chief Byers stepped forward. "I'm sorry. This does seem like the wrong time, and I'm afraid I don't understand all of it. But I would like to get some things straightened out."

"Has Muffin been in some trouble?" her mother wanted to know.

The Police Chief smiled. "Not trouble, exactly. But things are a bit mixed up."

Muffin was not going to be put off. Once more she pointed right at Mr. Bullen. "It's not mixed up. He stole my costume and stole Chris's magic bike."

"Let's take one thing at a time," pleaded the Chief. "In order. What's all this about a costume?"

I ran to the car, got out the warlock costume, and held it up so he could see. "We found this up in Mr. Bullen's yard with a trophy for the best costume. It belongs to Muffin. It was stolen from her."

"Oh dear, no," sighed Muffin's aunt. She said it in such a way that we all turned to her.

"I certainly didn't expect to see *that* again," she said, looking toward the adults. She seemed a bit embarrassed.

"Could you explain that?" my mother asked her.

"You know how Muffin does chatter about

magic," said the aunt. "It's really not right as far as I'm concerned. Goes on far too much. When she made up her Halloween costume, a witch, and a man witch at that, I just decided it wasn't right for her to be out looking that way. So I . . . gave it away."

"To whom?" asked the Chief.

"Why . . . why to that boy over there," and she pointed her finger right at my brother Mike.

Mike was sort of slumped over by the car. When Muffin's aunt pointed to him, he looked up and tried to smile, but he didn't quite do it.

"Michael," said my mother slowly. "Is that true?"

"It wasn't my fault," he said in a voice that was hard to hear.

"*What* wasn't your fault?" she demanded.

"You see," he said, "I was just walking around after school that day. And this lady—I never saw her before—called me over and said, 'Would you like a costume for Halloween?' I said 'sure,' so she gave it to me. I had the idea of fooling Chris. He's always making such a fuss about costumes, and secret identities, you know. So on Halloween night I put it on out in our shed. Then I came back and knocked on our door." He finally started to smile. "He didn't know who I was at all."

"Then you went to the parade?" I asked.

"I didn't really mean to do that either," he said. "I was walking away when I saw the parade starting to line up. I was just standing there, somebody handed me a number, said I should march . . ."

"And you won!" cried Eddie.

"Guess I did," said Mike. "It really was kind of an accident. When the Mayor gave me the prize I didn't want to say who I was, cause then Chris would have known."

"What about the bike?" my mother said very angrily. "Did you take that too?"

"No, honest, I didn't. But that's why I got rid of the costume. Chris kept saying that it was the warlock who took it. That got me sort of upset, so that time, on Sunday, when we went to get him a new bike at Mr. Bullen's place, remember, I went with you. When you were picking one, I got rid of the stuff. I didn't think he'd ever find it," he concluded in a low voice.

"I bet you *did* take it," I said.

"Really, I didn't," he almost wailed.

"You did too! When I rode the bike home from Eddie's on Halloween I left it right outside the house. You took it when you had your costume on."

"That's not the way it was, Chris," said Eddie's mother, who had been listening to everything that was being said. "On Halloween night I drove you home. Don't you remember, you and Eddie sneaked into the kitchen to scare John and me. By that time it was so late I had to drive you home."

"And that's how you lost your jacket," said my mother.

"But Mr. Podler said he saw the warlock jump over him with the bike," I insisted.

"Mr. Podler sometimes sees strange things," put in the Chief. "Where did you leave your bike?"

"On the bridge, I guess," I said, beginning to feel a little silly.

"What's your jacket look like?" he asked.

My mother walked over to the car and pulled out my old, dirty jacket. It was checkered. And I guess it did look a little like the warlock's cape.

The Chief figured the rest of it out. "Mr. Podler probably saw the bike with your jacket on it, and thought it was someone. I bet he walked right into it and sent it crashing down into the water. That's what he meant when he said he saw it fly."

"But I saw the warlock going through the sky with the bike!" I suddenly remembered.

"And when we got the bike back her parents came back," Eddie joined in.

"What about my coat being a Druid coat?" asked Muffin.

Muffin's mother laughed. "I was going to ask you about that. Why did you take my coat? It's much too big for you."

"Don't tell them Muffin," I cried out quickly. "They don't believe anything anyway!"

I was right, the grownups weren't listening. My mother started talking to Muffin's mother. Her father was scolding his sister. The Chief and Mr. Bullen were telling jokes. Rosemary was taking pictures of us all. As far as they were concerned the whole mystery was over.

❧ As it turned out,

that was pretty much the end. Muffin moved back to her own home with her folks. We write letters and I'm going to visit her during summer vacation.

Eddie and I are still best friends.

My brother Mike keeps teasing me about how he fooled me, but I don't pay attention.

My mother thinks it's all a little funny.

The only one I could even try to talk about it with was my father. And even he tried to get me to change my mind.

"Where's that list of yours where you asked yourself all those questions?" he wanted to know.

I found it and brought it out.

"What's it say on the top of the paper?" he asked.

I read it—"WHO STOLE THE BIKE?"

"That's it right there," he pointed out. "The wrong question. We should have asked, 'WHERE IS THE BIKE?'"

Then he sat back the way he does. "Get your questions right before you get your answers wrong," as if I had never heard that before.

"We got Muffin's parents back, didn't we?" I reminded him.

"A coincidence," he insisted.

"What about that Druid coat? You don't see many of those around."

"There is no more magic," he said.

My father was looking at me, trying, I guess, to figure out what I was thinking. Most times, like I said, he could. But not that time. No way. I had my Green Lantern ring on. It was glowing. It really was. And he says there's no more magic. Maybe. Maybe not.

Avi, a librarian at Trenton State College, is also a storyteller, teacher of children's literature, bookbinder, and collector of old children's books. He comes from a family of writers and his twin sister is a poet.

Avi lives in Lambertville, New Jersey, with his wife, a weaver, and their two sons. He enjoys buying his children comic books so that he can read them.

His previously published books for children are *Snail Tale* and *Things That Sometimes Happen,* which he calls "a collection of short stories for short readers."